MW01248241

Me and the Tidy Tornado

Good Grief, Idaho, Volume 2

Jessie Gussman

Published by Jessie Gussman, 2021.

ME AND THE TIDY TORNADO

First edition. February 16, 2021.

Written by Jessie Gussman.

Me and the Tidy Tornado

Cover art by Julia Gussman[1]
Editing by Heather Hayden[2]
Narration by Jay Dyess[3]
Author Services by CE Author Assistant[4]

~~~

Listen to the professionally produced audio version of this book – for FREE – HERE[5] on the SayWithJay Voiceworks Channel on YouTube.

Support our efforts to bring you quality audio at a price that fits into everyone's budget – FREE – check out all the FREE Dyess/Gussman audios HERE[6] **and hit the "Subscribe"** button while you're there. Thanks so much!

~~~

1. https://sweetlibertydesigns.com/services/

2. https://hhaydeneditor.com/

3. https://www.youtube.com/c/SaywithJay

4. http://www.ceauthorassistant.com/

5. https://www.youtube.com/watch?v=jyVE-U7JS1I&list=PLMynUTDTX-HZp6oYB1m7GCFxtkTUJWH7KT&index=2

6. https://www.youtube.com/c/SaywithJay

Chapter 1

Tammy

I should have bought a dog.

I stare at the large, masculine building housing the ATV dealership twenty minutes outside of my hometown of Good Grief, Idaho.

I don't know what I'm even doing here. I must have lost what little mind I had left after my marriage dissolved.

My ex liked to play mind games, only he never played by the rules.

Are there even rules for mind games?

Regardless, I'm a stickler for rules.

I never color outside the lines.

Except I'm standing in front of Foursquare ATV Sales and Service, and I'm definitely making a big loop outside the lines.

Huge.

Unheard of.

I borrowed my dad's truck.

He gave me an odd look when I asked if I could.

Of all his four daughters, I'm not exactly the one he'd expect to ask to borrow his truck.

Kori wouldn't need ask; she has her own.

It wouldn't be completely unheard of for Claire, and even Leah, who is a girly girl.

Me?

What in the world do I need a truck for?

I'm an English teacher.

My idea of a good time is hanging out at my sister's house, correcting papers while the hubbub of her and her two children flow around me.

Because my home is too quiet now that my husband left and took my boys with him.

Talk about having your heart broke.

I mentioned I was an English teacher. And yes, I know the grammar is incorrect in that last line.

That's why I decided to get a dog. Because I stopped caring.

What does it matter if I speak correctly?

It seems to be a stumbling block to people because they see me as straightlaced, serious, a stick-in-the-mud, no fun.

At least, that's what my ex said.

I straighten my purse over my shoulder, run my hand down my carefully pressed slacks, and wonder if maybe I should have changed out of my two-inch heels before I stopped at the store.

I hadn't even thought about it.

The wind ruffles my blouse as I hesitate for just a moment before deciding it doesn't matter what I wear.

People aren't going to be judging me for my clothes, and even if they do, there's nothing wrong with my outfit.

I look okay, I think.

But then, I lost twenty pounds after my husband left. I'm straight as a stick.

It wasn't the diet plan I would have chosen, but I don't regret the twenty pounds, and I suppose I could say good riddance to my ex too.

I just miss my boys.

My stomach churns.

I don't know why I'm nervous. It's not like I've never bought anything before.

I'm not going to finance it. I have plenty of money in the bank, and I'm going to write out a check.

There is nothing to be nervous about.

I walk in, and heat blows down as I pass through the doorway. The smell of oil and grease and garage hits me. Unfamiliar but not pleasant, and I wrinkle my nose.

You'd think they'd put some air fresheners or something in here.

I catch a whiff of cigarette smoke as well. I don't plan on being here long enough to worry about secondhand smoke. But I'll have to have my clothes dry-cleaned, because I can hardly show up in my English classroom reeking of cigarette smoke and garage smell. I probably ought to plan on sending my purse as well.

Maybe that is part of my problem. Maybe it doesn't matter what I smell like. Maybe it's not as bad as I think.

No. I will not listen to that voice. It's becoming louder in my head, and I absolutely am not interested in doing anything that my ex said I should.

There are what seems like dozens of four-wheelers sitting on the spacious floor. But no people in sight. The place looks deserted. Isn't there anyone here?

I'm getting ready to take a step toward the ATVs on display when something zips by my feet. I almost fall.

I think at first it is a dog, or maybe the Lord is sending me a sign that I need to turn around and leave the place immediately and go find someone who is selling puppies.

Any kind of puppy.

But my eyes focus, and I realize it's one of those monster truck toys. Remote controlled.

Where is the person holding the control? I look around the store. I can see someone in the far corner, through a door—maybe that's where the garage smell is coming from—working on what looks like a motorcycle.

I don't know anything about motorcycles, but this one has a low seat and high handlebars, and it sparkles like a Christmas tree, even though there are no lights on it. Whatever it is, it's fancy and looks expensive.

I don't want anything fancy, and I'm not buying a motorcycle. I am going to buy an ATV. I'm not sure I am going to drive it.

One step at a time. I take a breath. I can do this.

I step forward, and out of nowhere, the truck comes again, zipping between my legs.

I almost kick it, because I certainly am not expecting it.

I realize it's been humming around for a while, and I've been ignoring it.

I look around again. Whoever is playing with the toy will probably be in big trouble with his boss when I mention it to him.

A kid wearing a T-shirt and dirty jeans comes out from another door at the far wall, wiping his face with his hands before wiping his hands on his jeans. He's chewing like maybe I interrupted his lunch, even though it's afternoon.

The humming hasn't stopped, and he's not holding a controller, so I assume it's not him.

I stop again, waiting.

I don't recognize this kid, but that's not too surprising.

My hometown of Good Grief, Idaho, doesn't have an ATV shop, so I've driven halfway to Ravens Point, which is forty minutes away.

I don't do much business in Ravens Point, and I don't know anyone there.

My mouth is open, but I haven't said anything, when the truck that's been driving around bounces into my toe.

The words I had intended aren't what comes out.

"Take me to your supervisor," I say, my tone frosty. This is the part of me that I don't like. I don't mean to be frosty. I don't mean to be cold, and I definitely don't mean to be a straightlaced, serious witch.

Guess you know who said that.

Yes. My ex.

But it's my default mode. My protection mode. I don't smile or show happiness easily. I can't let loose. I can't goof off.

I used to be able to. My ex is wrong about that. But after he left, I knew he was right—I have a tendency to be too serious. I have a tendency to not let go, and maybe it's my teacher instincts, where I am constantly correcting children all day, telling them to behave, to pay attention, to not goof off, but I know that I have these tendencies.

I think it comes with being the oldest.

Regardless, it got worse after he left.

By design. I figure if he was going to leave me because I was too serious and straightlaced, then I want to make sure that if anyone else is ever interested in me, they understand what my personality is.

That, and cold and frosty aren't my emotions. They are the wall hiding my emotions.

I do that now because it's dangerous to allow people to see what I really feel. That's where the hurt happens.

I lift my chin as the boy stares at me with his mouth open. Apparently, not too many people walk in here and ask to see the supervisor.

I know I didn't stutter, so I wait for him to get with the program.

"Uh... I guess. You from the government?"

It's my turn to stare. What in the world would make him think that?

I don't worry the question too long in my brain. Sometimes, people just don't make sense. Especially teenage boys. This is one of those times.

"No. I need to speak with him. Immediately." He is going to get a piece of my mind over slacking employees who play with toys and run them into customers.

But I don't need to explain all of that to this kid. He just works here.

"Oh, okay. He's up there."

He points to the far wall, only up.

I turn, looking. I hadn't even noticed there is an overhang and what I assume are one-sided glass windows overlooking the store.

The kind of windows where he can see us but we can't see him.

I look both ways and don't see steps.

"How do I get there?"

The kid points over toward the door I'd noticed earlier through which I'd seen the man working on the motorcycle. The stairs run the far side of that door, tucked against the wall.

"Thank you," I say, and I pause, waiting for him to supply his name. He doesn't.

He just says, "You're welcome." And he walks off.

I try to impart manners into the children I teach every day.

I teach English, but that doesn't mean that I can't teach manners and common courtesy along with it.

I tried to instill them in my boys, too.

That was one thing their father was very good at. Being courteous. Except when he was insulting me.

The kid scratches behind his ear as he walks away.

The truck that had stopped against my toe backs up and does circles around me.

I'm annoyed. Seriously. Someone needs to stop this.

And then I think, why don't I laugh about it?

What's it hurting?

True, it isn't hurting anything.

But it is disrespectful and demeaning. I won't put up with it.

And now, instead of buying an ATV, I march angrily across the floor, not even looking at the four-wheelers that are sitting there as I pass them, eager to tell on someone and get them in trouble.

No wonder my husband didn't like me.

I don't even like myself at this moment.

Still, this is such egregiously unacceptable behavior I have to report it.

Although, if those are really single-sided windows, he might already be able to see.

A thought strikes me that is so compelling I almost stop.

Maybe he *has* seen it. Maybe he's okay with it.

I don't stop. It couldn't possibly be true.

I adjust my purse strap again, put my hand on the railing, and climb the metal stairs, my high heels clicking on the steps and reverberating throughout the store. This is just a simple warehouse building with a concrete floor and a ceiling showing exposed metal beams and ductwork. Nothing fancy. Of course, it's an ATV outlet, so it doesn't need to be.

It just needs to appeal to...men.

Maybe the truck appeals to men too.

My ex is a marketing exec in a big firm, but this whole thing would appeal to him for sure. The smell of the garage, the plainclothes building, even the remote-control truck.

There's no sign or anything on the door when I get to the top of the stairs, and I don't know whether I should knock or just walk in.

I decide to be bold.

That's the opposite of my usual decision.

I open the door and walk into a large open room—open from one end of the building to the other.

Right in the middle of the room, halfway down, there's a desk.

There's no one behind the desk. But there is a man sitting in an office chair, his feet propped up somehow on the window, facing me, and smirking.

Somehow, it doesn't surprise me to see that he is holding a remote control.

Chapter 2

Justin

Wow.

I've never seen anyone quite like this in my store before.

She obviously doesn't belong, but there's something so compelling about her that I haven't been able to stop looking at her since she walked in.

I suppose, if I were a smart man, I would have hidden the remote control before she walked in.

I'm a business owner and successful—this isn't the only business I own, but it's my latest venture, and I'm working my butt off to get it off the ground.

ATVs are a big sell in Idaho, and I can make this work.

Just like I've made my chain of gas stations and convenience stores work, and I even own a large cattle ranch in South Dakota that has been extremely successful.

It's not a matter necessarily of knowing your business inside out.

It's a matter of having people work for you who know your business inside out.

All of my businesses are profitable. Including this one.

I'm on the verge of handing it over; I just haven't found the right person yet.

And watching the lady striding toward me, I'm glad I haven't.

If her nose were any higher in the air, she'd have to put a little roof over it so she wouldn't drown when it rains.

Her high-heel shoes and fancy clothes look completely out of place in my shop, but they look good in a way, too.

She looks classy and she walks gracefully, even if she is sort of stomping, and her bone structure is fine, delicate almost, and makes every male part of me ache to protect her.

I almost snort over that.

It is the rest of the world that needs protection from this woman.

My parents taught me manners, but I don't stand up when she stops in front of me.

I smirk instead.

Yeah. She didn't have steam coming out of her ears before, but my smirk does the job.

She's officially well and truly jacked at me.

I like it.

Normally, I don't pick on people just to make them angry, but this woman looks so regal and queenly there's just a part of me that admires that and at the same time wants to push it and see her lose some of that outer shell, because obviously, there's a very passionate woman underneath.

I'm intrigued.

I do, however, remember that just because I'm intrigued doesn't mean she is.

That thought is disappointing, so I ignore it.

"I was told the supervisor is up here. I assume he stepped out?" Oh yeah, even her voice sounds elegant and refined.

Now, I've started and run a lot of businesses.

I'm not a billionaire or anything, but I've made a lot of money, and I've been successful. But my heart has always been in the outdoors.

I'm an Idaho man and proud of it. When someone looks at me, they don't think, "oh, there's a guy in touch with his feelings."

They probably think I am a candidate for therapy.

Maybe they're right.

I don't give a flip about my feelings, but honest-to-goodness, when she spoke, heat traveled the whole way up my spine and lapped around my rib cage, and I had the weirdest sensation of coming home.

Never felt anything like that before in my life.

I wouldn't mind feeling it again though. I like it.

"You'd assume wrong, ma'am," I say, and for a moment, I consider not dropping my feet and standing up.

But I feel like I'm a little at a disadvantage, because this woman is exceptionally thin and also very tall.

I drop my boots to the floor—I don't usually do it in quite such an abrupt way, but they fall loudly, echoing in the cavernous room—before I stand, slowly, enjoying the way her eyes move from looking down to looking up.

A woman of her height probably is not used to looking up to too many people.

I grin to myself. Maybe it's childish to want at least one little thing over her, but it makes me feel good. After all, she's outclassed me just by gracing me with her presence. My height is one little thing I have.

And I need to be grateful to the good Lord for that, because I certainly didn't do anything to grow this tall.

"I guess you're looking for me then," I drawl, enjoying the widening of her eyes and the way her mouth drops. Not the way someone else's mouth might drop, but just a graceful little O, perfect in its shape.

Davey had texted me and told me a lady was on her way up. I could see it. But he'd also said she wasn't a government official.

I can see why he asked.

That's my first thought.

I hold my hand out, wondering if she'll take it. "I'm Justin Gabriel, owner of Foursquare."

She was surprised before. Double that now.

Still, every feature looks perfect, not a hair out of place either. I don't even think her breathing shifted. But I know she is surprised.

"Tamera Fry," she says, taking my hand with hers. Her fingers are long and slender, and I bet if we hold our hands up together, hers will not be very much smaller than mine. I like that too.

I haven't seen much I don't like.

"Well, Mr. Gabriel," she says my name in that teacher's tone where a kid knows he's in deep, deep trouble, "I was coming up here to lodge a complaint about the employee who was playing with a toy instead of working."

Her nose moves—I'm not sure exactly how she did it, but it looked graceful, if noses can move in graceful ways—and one eyebrow arches up. I mean way, *way* up.

She continues, "But obviously, I wasted my time." Somehow, she manages to look down at me even though I am towering above her. "I was going to purchase an ATV from your store," she says, "but now I'm trying to figure out how close the next nearest dealership is."

"It's two hundred miles away, ma'am. That's why I started this one. ATVs are popular in Idaho, and there wasn't anything around. We also service them and motorcycles. So you buy here, you can bring it back to get it fixed if it needs it. Although if you buy new, you have a warranty." My words are slow and drawn out. I guess I just never learned to talk fast. I don't see any need to start now, even if she does have me a little excited. Not in a weird way, just in a I-see-a-beautiful-woman-that-I'm-attracted-to kind of way.

The attraction is clearly one-sided.

I'm fine with that. I've got my son to raise anyway. And as attractive as this woman is to me, she's not the kind of woman that's going to want to do the things I do.

I know even if there were something between us, it would never work.

Still, sometimes there's a huge disconnect between the brain and the heart. That's my problem right now.

My brain has lots of logic, and every argument it's giving is absolutely one hundred percent correct.

But my heart is like a little kid who's got his fingers in his ears and saying "nananananananananana" and not paying the slightest bit of attention to logic and reason.

"Two hundred miles?" she asks, the faintest traces of surprise in her tone.

"A little over but what's a few miles among friends," I say with a grin which she does not return. If anything, she frosts up on me more.

She reminds me a little of a porcupine. If you see them walking around when no one's bothering them, you don't even know they have stickers. It's not until they're riled that they put them up. It's the instinct they do for protection.

I feel like she's put her stickers up, which for her is a frosty and haughty attitude, in order to keep from getting hurt.

Which makes me think she's been hurt before.

I don't think she notices that my knuckles whiten around the remote control I'm still holding. I don't like the idea of someone hurting her.

She looks tough and cool, cold and hard, but I am sure, without a shadow of a doubt, that she's soft underneath.

That's the part of her I want to protect.

"I knew I should have gotten a dog," she mutters to herself.

I'm too surprised at first that she's muttering, and her words don't register right away.

But when they do, I realize she actually was here to buy a four-wheeler.

Part of me wants to make the sale, but not enough that I would try to talk her into something she doesn't want.

I hate salespeople like that.

But if she wants to buy an ATV, and if she lives anywhere near here, this is her best bet.

I set the controller down on the desk. Deliberately. And then I look back at her. "Sorry about the remote-control truck. That was all me. Obviously. I'm sorry that it bothered you." I shove a hand in my pocket, because for some reason when she's standing in front of me like this, I want to touch her. "If you want me to call Stick 'Em ATV and tell them you're coming, I will. You better get going, if you want to get back over to our side of the mountain before the snow starts."

I haven't checked the weather forecast, but it is always snowing up on the mountain, so I figure I am safe with what I said.

Her lips purse, and a flash of uncertainty crosses her face before she straightens her shoulders and lifts her chin. "There's an ATV down on your floor I want to purchase. Should I speak to your salesperson? He seemed to be on his lunch break earlier."

"Eh, Davey is always eating. He knows his stuff, though. Grew up around quads and won't lead you astray."

"Fine. Thank you," she says, and she turns.

I don't want her to leave. Business is usually pretty slow in the afternoon. It should be picking up in another half an hour or so. So even though Davey really needs the practice, and she seems like a sure sale, for some odd reason, I fall into step beside her.

"But since you took the trouble to walk the whole way up here, I'll help you. We'll give Davey a break." I'll end up paying him a commission for the sale anyway, since I am taking his customer, but I can't help it.

She's not my type. She's not even close to being my type.

Not that I even have a type. Being that I've been raising Roy for the last few years, and before that, I'd been more interested in backpacking through the woods, climbing mountains, being outside in general and didn't really have time to do much with girls.

Women.

Tamera is definitely a woman, not a girl. It has nothing to do with her size or shape or age and everything to do with the way she carries herself and the way she acts.

I still can't believe I am walking beside her, going down, and taking a sale away from my salesperson, just so I can spend more time with her.

It isn't like me.

Still, I reach ahead of her and open the door. I am not a total Neanderthal.

Her brows lift gently, and her eyes, a gray with just touches of green in them, meet mine.

I don't know what she feels. I can't read anything in them, other than a slight surprise. I have no idea what that means.

I hope she doesn't see in mine that that warm feeling is back, times ten. If this is the way I feel around her, I know I'm going to have trouble watching her leave.

Even now, I have an idea, something I can say that, depending on the reason she's buying an ATV, could make sure I see her again.

We walk down the stairs. I follow her, and as we reach the bottom, I strive for a casual tone. "Where are you from?"

"I live in Good Grief. I'm an English teacher at the high school there."

I almost could bet money on the fact that she's not buying this ATV herself. Probably an expensive birthday gift for one of her kids.

My eyes shoot to her hand.

Relief rushes, cool and fine, through me as I see there is no ring.

I can't believe I hadn't thought of that first.

I *always* think of that first.

I don't care how attractive she is, if she's married, she's not mine.

Even now, if there had been a ring on her finger, I would have handed her off to Davey. No questions asked. Definitely.

I am not that kind of man.

I have a lot of faults, but adultery has never been one of them.

"I live right on the edge of the school district line," I say, and I'm not sure why. She didn't ask and hasn't expressed any interest. I guess I'm just making conversation.

Because I want to find out more about her.

"What are you planning to do with your ATV?" I ask, trying to go into business mode and figure out which ATV would suit her.

"I haven't decided yet," she says, and then she stops beside our most powerful machine. "This is the one I want."

I can't help it. I blink multiple times, trying to process. Why would this slender, delicately regal woman want to purchase an ATV with that kind of power?

"Are you buying this for...your husband?" I didn't even want to say it, but I might as well find out now. I hold my breath until she answers.

"No. It's for me."

If she had balled up her elegant fingers and punched me in the stomach, I wouldn't have been more surprised than I was just then. "That's a pretty powerful machine. Is there a reason you chose this one?"

"Yes. Of course. Because of the color."

I cough. A lot. Because I wanted to laugh, belly laugh, because she's such a woman.

Of course, she wants to buy it because of the color. It's a powder blue, the color of a distant mountain on a snowy January day, as the clouds part and the sun shines down on it, just a natural, wild color that is still so close to baby blue it gives you peace when you look at it.

I actually love the color, but I would never buy a machine because of it.

"So you've driven a lot of ATVs?" I ask, but I'm pretty sure I know the answer. If she's picking an ATV because of the color...

"No, I've never driven one. But I intend to start. As soon as I get this home. I have a truck out in the parking lot." She reaches into her purse and pulls out a checkbook. "Who do I make the check out to?"

I fumble in my head, trying to remember the name of the company I started and pay the bills for every day.

I've never made a sale quite like this before. Ever. Not even close to one like this.

I finally find my brain and rattle off the name of my company, wondering if it's ethical for me to take her check. She's never even driven an ATV before, and she's going to pull out of the lot with this for herself.

Was she kidding me?

"So this is really for you?" I ask, feeling stupid, because she's already answered that question, but I just can't believe her.

"Yes." The way she says the word and the way she looks at me, with that eyebrow raised up to the sky again and that look in her eye, half challenging, half begging for my help, I just can't.

"So do you have property on which to run it?"

She doesn't answer until she finishes writing out the name on the line of the check. "I don't."

"I see."

I'm still trying to figure out how to piece this puzzle together, because something's not adding up, when she says, "Are you going to tell me how much it is? Is there tax on it? Should I just write out the amount on the tag?"

She was gonna write out a check for almost fifteen thousand dollars. I want to ask if it's going to bounce.

Maybe that's the catch. She's actually a crook.

I look at her again. Great disguise.

I wouldn't have suspected that ever, except this situation is just too weird.

"Do you need help, Mr. Gabriel?" Davey asks from my side. I never even heard him come. He startles me, and I struggle not to jump.

"I've got this, thanks, Davey. If no one else comes in, you can shelve that inventory that's sitting on the skid in the back."

"Yes sir, Mr. Gabriel." Davey turns and heads toward the back room.

"If you would walk over to the counter with me, I'll figure up the tax and the license fees, and a couple other things that I'll have to add to that. I'll itemize it for you at the computer. And give you a printout."

She nods, regally, and I just can't get over that I can even be attracted to someone like this.

But the attraction and the attractiveness is only part of it. I feel like she needs to be protected. I want to do that for her.

Weird.

I walk over after grabbing the tag, and she follows me. Normally, I go over on the other side of the counter and stand up at my computer, working that way, but contributing to the craziness of the situation, I turn the computer to face me and stand in front of the counter with her beside me. It's what I wanted, and I have to admit it feels right that she's there.

She watches what I do, and I kinda feel like she's checking to make sure I do it right.

I'm going to hand her a printout. There's no chance of me cheating her, but it's okay, I don't mind her standing this close and looking over my shoulder.

Truth be told, I like it.

I ask all the typical questions, if she wants insurance or the warranty. I explain the factory warranty and then the add-on, which she declines. I feel that is the best choice, but I don't say it. I actually make more money if she buys the warranty.

But I never try to talk my customers into it. To me, that's wrong.

She declined it before I could tell her I didn't think it was worth the money.

I do, however, remind her that we have a shop, and we do warranty work there.

"Do you do the work, Mr. Gabriel?" she asks, and it almost seems like a challenge.

"I can. And I have. But I have a mechanic too. And you can call me Justin."

"Mr. Gabriel is fine," she says, not unkindly but not in a friendly way, either.

"All right, Tamera, I'm going to print out some papers for you, and there will be a few things for you to sign."

She notices my use, deliberate use, of her first name, but she doesn't have a bad reaction.

Maybe that was a little bit of a smile tickling around her mouth.

Her lips do not work up though. Not even a little.

I really, really want to see her smile, but I know I can't be a businesslike salesperson and also make her smile.

Normally, I can joke with customers, and I do. But Tamera is different, and she kind of makes me feel like I need to take life more seriously than what I do.

She's probably right.

Although, what's the fun in that?

Maybe, maybe I *should* be the one to make her loosen up.

I wonder if that's even possible.

It would be quite a challenge.

I like challenges.

Chapter 3
Tammy

I'm not typically tempted to fidget, but I'm fighting the urge right now.

The man doesn't make me nervous exactly, but he makes me feel odd. I can't put my finger on when I've ever felt like that before, and it's not completely uncomfortable, but it's weird in a good way.

It makes me want to move.

The really odd thing is it makes me want to move closer. To him.

I've spent the years since my divorce moving further away from men.

I know my frosty personality is dialed up on high, and it doesn't seem to be putting him off.

Of course, I'm spending upwards of fifteen thousand dollars in his store, so maybe he's being nice to me despite the fact that I'm doing everything in my power to be an ice princess.

He hands me some papers. I force myself to focus on reading and signing.

I still can't believe I've almost done it. He asked some very legitimate questions, and I answered honestly, even though they made me feel stupid.

I don't have any place to ride my ATV. Why in the world am I buying one?

His finger comes down, on the paper, and his hand fascinates me again.

I'm tall for a woman, and typically, most men I meet I look down on.

Especially with the two-inch heels I'm wearing. It puts me over six feet.

He's taller than I am, for one, which of course I like. Although, it does put me at more of a disadvantage, because I'm definitely not used to it.

But his fingers are long and somehow graceful for a man, and even though he seems to have an office job, they're brown with scars on them.

It makes me curious about him. He must do something outside in his spare time.

I shouldn't care.

I *don't* care.

He hands me a pen, and before I sign my name, I say, "I'm sorry, what did you say this was for?"

"In case of an accident, you're willing all of your worldly possessions to me. Just sign right here." He tapped the paper.

I have the pen poised above the paper, and I'm looking at the line, but it's faded away. I'm trying hard not to smile.

I know that's not what the paper says.

I can't let him get to me.

Somehow, a smile shows weakness. It's emotion. And I'm not going to let him know because somehow, someway, he can use that to hurt me.

Actually, I know those are scars from my ex.

But I don't want to chance it again.

I straighten my features before I look up.

"Mr. Gabriel, I assume that's your idea of a joke?" My voice is nothing but frost. His eyes don't even flicker though. In fact, my question makes him smile.

"Excuse me, ma'am. I couldn't resist." He doesn't explain further, and I don't ask what it is that he can't resist.

I'm sure it's not me. But I'm not sure what it could be.

I assure myself I don't care.

"So, what does the paper say?" I ask again.

Then I shake my head. Why am I asking?

"Never mind." I tug it out from underneath that finger that I can't help but admire. "I can read it for myself."

"You don't have to. It's just stating that you're refusing the additional warranty, and you understand what the factory warranty covers, which I've already explained to you."

Indeed, as I skim over it, that's exactly what the paper says.

I put it down and sign my name.

He watches me and then looks at my signature for a couple of minutes after I'm done.

After my divorce, I wanted to change my name back to my maiden name, but I've never gotten around to it.

I don't want to carry that man's name, but I also don't want to put that kind of effort into cutting him out of my life.

I hate that he has any kind of sway over me at all.

"Here's another one. This is the one that says you give me permission to come to your house anytime I want to and ride the ATV, as long as I fill it up with gas when I'm done."

I looked down quickly, because that did make the corners of my mouth quirk.

I sigh, a put-out sound that I'm confident assures him that I'm annoyed and not amused.

I don't look up until my face has straightened. I tug the paper out from underneath his finger while holding his eyes.

"I'll read this one for myself too," I say with a smug look that conveys superiority.

That's what I intend anyway.

This one states that I'm purchasing a license from the state of Idaho, and I understand the license needs to be renewed on a yearly basis.

I sign.

Again he watches. He seems almost fascinated with my signature. Which seems odd. But then the thought hits me.

Could he be watching my hand?

I am fascinated with his.

I shake my head at myself, careful not to do it so he can see. Of course he's not interested me. Of course he's not watching my hand.

Of all the ridiculous ideas I've ever had...

Even if he were, I don't care. This is not the kind of man I want to have anything to do with.

Granted, he's nothing like my ex, but he's still a man and annoying at that.

I take my hands off the paper, and he slides it away.

He sets another one down, but before he can say anything, I say, "And I suppose this one is where I agree to give you access to my house, including my kitchen and my refrigerator, which I'm also agreeing to keep stocked full of all of your favorite foods at all times." I look up at him, and I raise my brow, which, I might say, is usually a pretty effective look for me. "We're not getting married, Mr. Gabriel. I'm buying a four-wheeler from you." I lift the paper up and read it myself.

Actually, I pretend to read it, because I've surprised him, and he doesn't know whether to laugh or whether to keep looking at me with bug eyes.

He does both, grunting with his eyes popped open.

I want to tell him he looks ridiculous like that, but I don't want to be mean. And I definitely don't want to hurt his feelings. He might not understand I'm joking.

He doesn't look ridiculous. He looks cute.

I set the paper down, and I sign my name.

I have no idea what I just agreed to.

He takes the paper and begins to read, "To whom it may concern: I agreed to pay Mr. Gabriel the sum of one thousand dollars per day for the privilege of tutoring his son who is failing English. By paying Mr. Gabriel the sum of one thousand dollars per day, I guarantee him that his son will pass tenth-grade English, even if I have to falsify his records."

My cheeks are hot. They have to be bright red. My breath is shallow.

I honestly hadn't read that paper. It very well could say that.

I am too embarrassed to admit that I have no idea whether he is actually teasing me or whether he is serious.

"I didn't think you were actually reading them," he says in that slow drawl that flows like warm honey across my skin. I do not shiver. I refuse to.

I lift my chin, knowing that if that's what the paper actually says, I am in some hot water.

I live very frugally and never spend anything. Somehow, being alone scares me that everything is on me.

When a person is married, they have a little bit of a safety net. Someone to care for you if something happens. Two incomes. Two people to carry the load. Two opinions. And of course, sometimes those opinions disagree, and strongly, but it happened so many times that my ex would see things that I didn't.

Now that I'm alone, I only have mine, and I'm embarrassed to say how often I'm wrong.

Anyway, while I'm frugal, I don't have that kind of money.

He tortures me just a little bit longer before he holds the paper up, both hands at the top, gripping it with the thumb and his first finger, and then slowly the paper starts to rip. He tears it in half.

He hands half to me. "This is yours. Don't lose it."

"Thank you. I will take it home and burn it."

"Watch the smoke detectors, and don't burn your house down. That's kind of shooting your nose to spite your face."

"In your opinion, maybe. In my opinion, it might be worth it."

The thought strikes me that if Mr. Gabriel and I were in the same house together, there would be a wide and ongoing difference of opinion on probably almost everything.

I'm not entirely sure that's a bad thing.

My ex and I agreed on everything, except me.

At the end, he hated me. Most of the time, I don't hate myself.

Although, most of the time, I know I can be better.

I wish I were brave.

If I were brave, I would smile at this man and flirt with him. Maybe we'd go out to dinner and have a fun evening together.

It wouldn't mean anything, but maybe I'd let him kiss me at the end of it, just because I was brave.

I realize I want to.

I take a deep breath and set the pen down, careful to keep it perpendicular with the edge of the counter.

I brush my hands together and turn and face Mr. Gabriel. "Is that everything?"

"It sure is. I've got to get the key. I'll slop some gas in that for you, and you can drive it out of here."

He smirks at me, almost as though he knows the panic his words have created in my chest.

I have no idea how to drive it. And I don't want to learn in front of him.

He's already started to turn, but I say, "That's okay. You can drive it out. I'll hold the door for you."

"There's no need, we actually have a garage door, and I'll open that up."

His eyes twinkle with a devilish look that is also devilishly handsome.

Not a look I'm normally attracted to.

"Are you sure you don't want to drive it yourself, Tammy?"

My mouth opens. I gave him my given name, Tamera, just to be as formal as possible. He deliberately used it earlier, and now he's shortened it even more.

It's the name I go by, Tammy. It's what my sisters call me, my parents, and everyone.

Except my students who call me Mrs. Fry.

I lift my chin, refusing to take his bait. "I'm sure. I will allow you to ride it this one time."

"All right then. I'll get everything together."

He walks away from me, and I'm unsure of what to do.

I just bought myself a nice blue four-wheeler that I have absolutely no idea how to operate.

I'm assuming there are instructions somewhere. I can read English—after all, I'm an English teacher—and I can figure this out. Myself. I do not need Mr. Gabriel to help me.

I actually wouldn't mind having him help me.

Mr. Gabriel has disappeared out in the shop where I saw the man working when I first came in, so I debate about going out to my dad's truck and just waiting there, but I wander over to the four-wheeler and look it over more closely.

Where am I going to ride this thing? And why exactly did I buy it in the first place?

Maybe, if my divorce had just been happening, or if I'd been going through it, maybe I could explain this away. But that was years ago.

Is this a midlife crisis?

I am only in my mid-forties.

What is the age at which a person has a midlife crisis?

I don't feel like I am having a midlife crisis, but I honestly don't know.

I do feel restless, but I hadn't before I came in.

For goodness' sake, I held Jello, my sister's dog, while the girls' basketball team locked my sister in the control room with her co-coach and neighbor, and although I felt a little longing to have a dog of my own, I've ended up with a four-wheeler.

I'm not sure how things got so out of hand. Usually, I'm much more methodical than this.

I think about my mom saying, *God has a plan, and everything happens for a reason.*

I look around the large warehouse-type building at all the different four-wheelers sitting there, shelves of parts, whatever they are.

I don't even like riding four-wheelers. At least, I don't think I do, since I've never actually ridden one.

And yet I'm standing here, feeling like this is what I should do, even if I have no clue what I'm doing.

It's insane the way life goes sometimes. It's extremely nuts to watch yourself, almost like an out-of-body experience, as you do something you never would have done and wonder why.

I have the power to stop it. I am pretty sure I can change my mind. I think Mr. Gabriel would hand me my check back or rip it up. Pretty sure.

But I don't want to. I want to go and see this through, even if it is just taking the four- wheeler off the truck and parking it in my front yard and looking at it every day as I walk to my car to go to work. And every night when I come home.

Chapter 4

Tammy

"Hello?"

I jerk out of my thoughts, realizing that Mr. Gabriel has said something to me and I've missed it.

The key to the four-wheeler is dangling in front of my face, and I assume he must have asked if I changed my mind about driving out.

"You go ahead. I don't want to hit anything." And yes, there's a little bit of sarcasm in my voice as I think about his remote-control truck crashing into my foot.

I think that's a flicker of embarrassment that crosses his face, but it's really hard to tell.

He's tall and dark, with eyes so brown they look black.

He has facial features that make me think maybe he has some type of Native American blood in his background.

His nose is strong and straight, other than a knot that says it might have been broken at one point, and speaks of European ancestors as well.

I don't know why I am even looking. I don't care.

I turn my eyes away from the key, and he drops it to his side, walking over and straddling the four-wheeler like he's done it a million times, putting the key in the ignition, clicking a couple buttons, and starting it.

"I'm going quickly, because I don't want to sit here and let the fumes fill the building," he says, and I assume it is out of consideration for me, before he drives out.

I appreciate that.

I follow him out the garage door, and Davey appears behind me, closing it from the outside and picking up two long boards. He follows me across the parking lot.

It isn't hard to tell which vehicle is mine, since it is the only one in the lot.

I suppose, when a person pays fifteen thousand dollars for something, Mr. Gabriel and his store gets a rather large chunk of that. They probably don't need to sell too many in order to make their lease payment. Or whatever it is that they need to keep the building.

I hope it isn't much, because the building isn't much to speak of.

Regardless, Mr. Gabriel stops the four-wheeler beside my truck and opens the tailgate. I never even considered how he would get the four-wheeler inside of it, but Davey puts the boards down, and they adjust them to the width of the four-wheeler before Mr. Gabriel looks at me with a grin.

"Change your mind? Want to take it up?"

"No, thank you," I say automatically. Another thought strikes me.

The first time I drive an ATV, I'll have to pull it off my dad's truck.

I correct myself as he pulls onto the truck. I'll have to *back* it off.

I wonder what my dad will say if I return his truck with a four-wheeler on the back.

Poor Dad. He spent a good piece of his adult life in a house with five women.

Going to work at the vet clinic he owned was probably like entering a sanctuary.

I can see him shaking his head and rubbing his hand over his thinning hair.

It is about time for him to retire, but he probably won't until my mom slows down a little.

I don't think Mom will ever slow down.

I can't imagine Mom doing any speed other than full throttle. I have to admit she makes an excellent fire chief.

I take after Dad.

Only English is my sanctuary, not an animal clinic.

Mr. Gabriel has shut the four-wheeler off, and instead of climbing down off the boards the way he'd come up, he puts a hand on the edge of the truck bed and jumps over it, landing beside it on both feet, uncomfortably close to me.

I step back.

I know I'm not supposed to be impressed. I know he is probably just showing off. But I don't care, and I am.

It's hard to judge his age; his eyes have crinkles at the corners, like he laughs a lot, and I believe he does.

The phrase weather-beaten seems to describe him, like he spends a lot of time outside, and that makes sense to me too.

His work boots are a little out of place as a business owner, and he's wearing a ball cap instead of a cowboy hat.

He seems younger, but I bet he's about my age.

Maybe he's older. I'm not sure.

I want to know.

"How old are you, Mr. Gabriel?" I ask, and I can hardly believe the words come out of my mouth.

I never ask people questions like that. I'm always extremely proper and polite.

"I'm four years older than you, only my birthday is at the end of March instead of the beginning."

I widen my eyes, and then I realize I had to give him my driver's license when he was registering the ATV.

He'd figured out my age.

And he remembered it, in comparison to his.

Maybe I am grasping at straws. I probably am. I have a tendency to do that.

"I thought you were older," I say and wish I hadn't said anything.

He grins like my comment doesn't bother him at all. "I thought the same thing about you."

I want to call him on that one. Because I know he's lying too.

But I don't. He could have called me out, and he didn't. Instead, he teases me like I deserve.

He holds his hand out as Davey slams the tailgate shut. The key dangles from his fingers. "Here you go. We're closing here in a couple hours, so if you tell me where you live, I'll come to your house and back off for you, if you want me to."

I know he's serious. Throughout the time we've spent together, he's had a twinkle in his eye or a smile hovering around his mouth. It just seems natural for him to tease me.

Normally, I'm not the kind of person that people tease. Typically, my carriage and my expression command respect.

I kind of like it, that he's not afraid of me.

But now I can tell he's serious. He wants to help.

I think he might be a little worried about me. The thought makes me smile.

"Thank you. I think I'd like that."

Chapter 5

Justin

I can't believe Tammy gave me her address.

Tamera actually suits her better, but I can't seem to stop myself from picking on her when she's near me. I want to see her smile. Maybe it's not the best way to go about it, but it's all I have.

Still, I wasn't teasing when I offered, although I didn't think she'd accept.

But I was pretty sure she wasn't going to be able to get the four-wheeler off the truck on her own, and she apparently was smart enough to figure that out, too.

Not smart enough, *humble* enough to admit it.

I'm pretty excited about going to Tammy's, and it has nothing to do with helping out a customer.

She actually lives right on the outskirts of Good Grief, which is about twenty minutes from my place right on the line between the Good Grief school district and the neighboring one.

I leave work early. We have two customers come in after Tammy, and they both make significant purchases.

But after that, business dies.

It'll be good for Davey to lock up. He knows how.

The shop closes earlier, so I don't have to worry about that.

I need to find someone to run this for me, to free myself up.

My other businesses pretty much run themselves, and I have great people in charge, but I need to stay on top of things.

I could hire someone for that too, but I enjoy doing it. I like to have my fingers in everything.

My son, Roy, is at home, and he really is struggling with English. From what he says, his teacher is draconian and demands way too much out of her students.

I'm all about making kids work. That is good for them, but there need to be some limits too.

Then again, it might be Roy adjusting.

He spent most of his life living with his mom. We split when he was not even in kindergarten yet.

I saw him every chance I got, taking time off from my businesses and buying expensive airline tickets to go wherever she was.

He seemed to get along okay with her first husband, but he spent some time with me during that divorce.

Then, the man who moved in with my ex a couple of months later didn't get along with Roy, who was about twelve.

It might have been Roy. That's a hard age. I'm not blaming the guy. I don't even know him.

I really don't care. If anything, I owe the guy a thank you, because he reunited me with my son.

I did thank my ex. My son was on the phone with me every night, begging to be taken out of the home, and while my ex had custody, she allowed him to make the decision to move out.

It might have had something to do with the fact that she was pregnant and didn't want the stress of a belligerent preteen boy in the house. I don't know. I didn't ask. I was just grateful that I got my son back.

That was three years ago, and he's done okay, but high school has been hard, and I haven't quite figured out why.

English is the worst. It's not exactly my best subject either.

He's managed to keep a passing grade all year, but he flunked his term paper, and while the teacher gave him the opportunity to rewrite it, that isn't going so well either.

He needs to get a really good grade on this in order to pass.

Normally, the bus drops him off at my shop after school, and he works on the floor on an as-needed basis, picking up any slack. Normally, we're busiest in the evenings.

When we're not busy, he does his schoolwork.

Roy had gotten off the bus at my house because of spending extra time on his English, so I check in on him on my way to Tammy's.

It's not completely unusual for me to visit a customer after a sale, and he doesn't question me when I say I am going to give a customer a hand with their new four-wheeler.

I ask him to turn the oven on and put the casserole we made the night before in.

I expect to be back in time to take it out myself.

I also have a thought. One that's a little crazy, but I've always liked a little crazy.

My GPS takes me right to her driveway, and she lives in a cute little house. Yellow, which is not the color I would have guessed. I might have said beige or white.

I like it though. It's pretty. And cheerful.

Her truck is parked in her driveway, and while she does have a yard, it's not big enough to ride a four-wheeler around in.

I don't know how far behind her house she owns, and it's dark, so I can't see anyway. She's right on the outside of Good Grief, and as far as I know, there's only one row of houses along each side of the street.

Maybe she was waiting for me, I don't know, but she's coming out of the door as I get out of my truck.

I didn't figure she'd invite me in.

Not that I could do it, with supper in the oven and Roy waiting on me at home.

I greet her with a smile and notice she's changed her clothes.

She looks a little less uptight in jeans and a sweater.

She has some kind of slip-on shoe on her foot. Maybe like a ballet shoe or something. I forget what my ex calls them.

She doesn't exactly return my smile, but her eyes seem to crinkle a little, and I almost give myself credit for that.

"Hey, Tammy. I see you've decided to go ahead and wait on me," I say, nodding at the pickup where the four-wheeler still sits in the back.

"I didn't want you to come all the way out here for nothing...even though I could have gotten it off myself."

"I'm sure you could have," I say, my tone saying I think anything but.

She acknowledges that with a slightly embarrassed look because she knows it's the truth. I give her that. Because after all, we don't want to admit to our incompetence, especially to a complete stranger and one that has been picking on her pretty hard to boot.

Speaking of, I say, "I just wanted to apologize for picking on you today. I don't usually do that to customers. I'm not sure why I did it today. I probably gave you a shopping experience you never had before, and while I didn't mean any harm by it, I'm sorry."

She looks at me, and there are three vertical lines between her brows. She tilts her head just a little. It's the most emotion I've seen out of her; she's obviously confused. "You just apologized."

I almost laugh, but I stop myself just in time. I don't know what her past is. I don't see any kids running around. Maybe she's never been married, or maybe she has a jerk ex, one who never apologized.

That's my guess.

I say, "Yes. I owed you one. And I gave it to you. If you spend any amount of time around me, I'm sure I'll owe you more. Hopefully, you'll get them. I try to pay what I owe."

She seems to notice that I'm not teasing.

I notice that she's kind of sensitive that way and picks up on my nonverbal cues pretty easily. Cues I don't even realize I'm giving, but apparently I am, because somehow she's figured me out.

I like that she's taken the time to do that. In my experience, most women don't.

Not that I have vast amounts of experience. I'd rather be alone with my backpack in the woods anyway.

"I appreciate that. Your apology is accepted. And, since you're such a good example...I know I wasn't exceptionally nice. I've never been in a shop like that before, and obviously, I'm sure you figured out I've never bought an ATV before, either. I was uncomfortable, and I covered it with something that came close to snobbery." She looks down, like she knows that's exactly what she did. But I hadn't considered that her attitude was a cover for her nervousness.

It makes total sense to me. I can tell she is a woman of strong emotion, and now it all makes sense. Probably, it feels safer to be unemotional than to be real.

I get that.

She looks back up. "I'm sorry."

She is completely sincere, and I believe her.

"Accepted. Although I don't feel there's a need for it." And that is true, because I don't. She hasn't hurt me; she just goaded me on to tease her even more, to try to get under her exterior.

I don't have to admit to everything.

"I figured I'd get this off for you and give you a little lesson on how to start it and run it, and..." I shove a hand into my pocket because I'm about to suggest the crazy thing I decided to do. Although now that it is time to let the words out, I'm not sure if I can back up my big thoughts with any kind of action.

Nothing ventured, nothing gained.

Chapter 6

Justin

"There's a charity run, two weeks from Saturday. I didn't know if you'd be interested in going. I can help you if you want. I've got a trailer, and I can come pick you and your machine up."

"A charity run?"

I nod, although I don't tell her that we often call it a poker run, because it's very similar, only instead of one person winning the pot, that person gets to pick from five or six charities and all the proceeds are donated to that.

Maybe poker runs are slightly more popular, but I doubt it.

Typically, poker runs are on Sunday, and even more typically, pretty much everyone is drunk.

That's information I keep to myself as well, because it doesn't apply to charity runs.

Not much anyway.

She's nodding her head, but I can tell she's gonna say no. So I start talking again. I've learned a little bit about sales since I bought the shop.

"We did them all last year. We quit before Christmas, but every single one went to a really good cause." I hook my hand around the back of my neck and try to make sure I word this in the best way possible. "I don't know if you've heard of Jill Powell, but she's a young mother of three children, and she's fighting pretty bad cancer. She has lots of medical bills, and her husband was laid off his job, since he worked in oil. When that came to a screeching halt, it put lots of guys out of work. Anyway, she lost her health insurance, and I think maybe half of the runs that we did last year we donated to that family. It ended up being over thirty thousand dollars. I know they were really able to use it."

I try not to be sappy but to put enough inflection in my voice to touch her heart.

I'm not manipulating her exactly, because every word of it was true. We really do give to good, local causes, but I *am* trying to influence her, and I have to admit that.

I want her to go.

I'm not even sure why.

Roy will be there, and we haven't talked about my son yet.

I don't think I'll do that tonight, either.

"Why haven't I seen you around?" she asks.

I wasn't expecting that question. "I don't know. You mean around Good Grief?"

"Yes. Around town at all?"

"I guess I work a lot." I don't know where she thought she'd see me in town. Good Grief had what? A church. The fire hall. And a tavern.

Unless she expects me to just drive into town and walk along the sidewalk every once in a while.

Maybe she does.

I drop my hand from around my neck and try to figure out how this could play into getting her to go to the charity run.

"So I guess the fire hall has dinners pretty often," I say. Fishing, because I have no idea what in the world she thinks I should be doing in Good Grief that she would actually see me.

"They do. The school has basketball games, and there are football games in the fall."

I hadn't even thought about the school. Roy hasn't shown any interest in going to any games, and I haven't suggested it. Sports are okay, but I'd rather be in the woods. When I have time. My businesses really do take up a good bit of it.

She narrows her eyes a little at me. "And yes, the fire hall has dinners. The church has services. And occasionally, I run into the tavern and pick up orders of fries. Normally when I go in, I know everyone there. I think I would remember if I saw you and didn't recognize you."

"I've heard the fries are really good. I should come around more often. We just moved here less than a year ago, and I guess I just haven't gotten with the social scene yet."

"You should."

I nod. "What do you suggest I start with?"

"There's a basketball game on Friday night. You could start with that."

"Are you going be there?" That was a pretty bold question, but she's pushing me pretty hard, and I like this version of her too.

She's a little more relaxed, which must be because she's in a comfortable environment, and she's challenging me.

I might have mentioned already: I like challenges.

"My sister and her fiancé coach the team. I try to make it to every game. Especially the home games."

"I'll be there Friday. I'll look for you."

It isn't exactly a date, but she invited me, and I accepted. We just aren't going together, unless I ask... I decide that's pushing too hard.

Plus, I wouldn't do that to Roy. My kid comes first.

She gives a little nod of her head, looking regal again. Funny how a woman can wear the fancy clothes, and it doesn't mask the fact that they're just bubbly and happy, almost to the point of being a goofball.

And yet Tammy can come outside in a pair of jeans and a casual sweater and look as regal as if she were wearing a ball gown with heels and gloves and crown and the whole nine yards.

"You never answered me about the charity run. What do you say?"

Hopefully, my easy acceptance with the basketball game will inspire her to say yes to the charity run.

"I need to think about it. How many people usually go?"

I try to keep the excitement off my face and out of my voice. She's thinking about it. That is more than I had hoped for. "I never counted.

And the course is pretty long, so even if there's a lot of people there, the machines are usually pretty spaced out."

"Spaced out how? What exactly happens again?"

"I don't think I told you. I just told you the good it does. You have to pay a fee to participate, which I would take care of since I invited you." I grin a little, to see if I can get a bit of a rise out of her. I'm not exactly calling it a date, but the man is paying.

She shakes her head just a little, and maybe her eyes twinkle. I can't be sure.

"Then you just start out and ride on the trail, and you pick up tokens at designated stopping points. There are twenty-four along the way. When you get back, you try to match your tokens up on the big board. The first one who gets five in a row wins. And they get to pick the charity we donate to."

"I see. So it's not really a race? You just have to go fast if you want to pick the charity, and even then if you win, you might not get to depending on the kind of tokens you get?"

"That's pretty much it, yeah." It is slightly more involved than that, but that is good enough for now.

"I see. So I can go as slow as I want to?"

"You can. And I'll ride with you, since it's your first time."

"Not everyone goes to race?"

"Most don't. Most people go just to have a ride in the woods. We can do that."

"You said 'since it is my first time.' Which makes me think that people don't normally go together."

"That's not true. I just never have." I definitely have a competitive side, but I usually go and enjoy the ride. But I've never hung around with someone other than Roy, who usually likes to race at the front. I like being by myself.

Although I won't mind at all being with Tammy. I'm not going to tell her that.

"I suppose I could try it," she says thoughtfully, as though she is pondering a great decision. Maybe it is for her. "As long as I can practice a little here in the yard first. But I think I can. You said two weeks from Saturday?"

"That's right." My heart's jumping up and down, giving my lungs a high five.

I'm so down for seeing Tammy the ice princess on the charity run trail.

I don't even question why I'm so excited. Maybe there's just something about sharing something you love with someone you're interested in.

I want to see her eyes light up and for her to love it too.

Yeah, maybe I am reaching a little high, but something tells me underneath that cool exterior, there is a passionate woman who will have a lot of fun on a charity run.

I sure hope so. For some reason, I haven't even spent that much time with her, and she's gotten under my skin. I want to spend more.

It looks like I am going to get to.

It doesn't take me any time at all to put the tailgate down, adjust the unloading boards, and back the four-wheeler off the pickup.

If I had been doing it myself, I would have backed up to a bank and gotten it off there, but I didn't even bother to look around for one here in the dark.

She thanks me, and I tell her I'll see her Friday night.

Her lip does quirk up, just one side, but it totally counts.

I honestly am looking forward to it.

Chapter 7

Tammy

I pull into my parents' house, kind of hoping they're already in bed and I can just park my dad's pickup and take my car home.

But there are lights on in the kitchen, and I know it will hurt their feelings if I leave without walking in and saying something.

So I do.

I was always taught, and I believe, you reap what you sow.

I don't know exactly what's gonna happen with my boys, but I've always tried hard to treat my parents the way I want my children to treat me.

After I got out of my teenage years, of course.

Not that I was ever rebellious as a teenager. My parents wouldn't have stood for that. Neither my mom nor my soft-spoken father.

I didn't appreciate them then, not like I did after I came back from college.

They supported me through my divorce.

That was probably the worst time of my life.

There's something about a man dumping you for someone else that just makes you feel worthless.

I'm over it now. Although the scars are real.

I think he's probably ruined me for anyone else. I don't think I can shed my ice princess persona and allow someone else the chance to devastate me the way my ex did.

Mom always says I'm stronger than I think I am, but I think she's wrong.

I don't think I'm as strong as people think I must be when they look at me.

Plus, at my age—which is closer to fifty than forty—risks seem more dangerous.

I feel like Jell-O inside, which reminds me of my sister's dog that she named Jello.

I walk straight into my parents' house without knocking. This house isn't even the one I grew up in, and yet it feels like my parents' house is mine.

What a weird feeling.

Anyway, my mom and dad are sitting at the kitchen table, and they both have ice cream in front of them.

I don't think they heard me pull in, and they are leaning across the corner of the table, and maybe my dad is whispering in my mom's ear, but I think they are kissing.

I know parents do all those things that married people do, but it's uncomfortable for me to think about.

I turn my eyes away and shut the door, possibly harder than necessary.

When I look back, they've thankfully broken apart.

I'm a little hard on them, but that's the way I wanted my marriage to be.

My mom is eccentric to say the least, but my dad adores her.

She might be odd, but my dad never wants for anything, and there's never been a question in my mind that my mom would do anything for him.

I've always respected my dad, and now that I'm an adult, I can see it's because my mom has always respected my dad.

I've never heard either one of them say a bad word about the other.

They make it look easy, but looking back at my own failed marriage, I know it's not.

Maybe I shouldn't avert my eyes and allow myself to get uncomfortable at all. After all, I'm sure that's part of what's made their marriage strong.

I suppose it's too late for me, but I have some wisdom and experience. Maybe I can help someone else.

I'm not sure who, since my boys don't even want me.

I can't think about that; it hurts too much.

"Tammy! We waited up because we knew you were coming." My mom jumps up and acts like she hasn't seen me in six months.

I just saw her in church on Sunday. Two days ago.

"That was nice of you, Mom. It's good to see you guys." My voice is slightly less enthused, but I appreciate my mom and return her hug.

My dad, more reserved, has stood up from his chair as Mom and I walk into the kitchen with her arm around my shoulders.

"Hey there, kiddo," my dad says. That's what he's always called me, and even though I feel like I might have outgrown the name by now, considering I'm looking pretty hard at fifty, when Dad calls me that, it always makes me feel like a kid again.

"Hey, Dad. I brought your truck back. I just dented it in a couple of different places, nothing you can't pound out with a hammer on Saturday afternoon. I'll come over and give you a hand if you want me to."

My dad narrows his eyes at me, like he's not sure whether to believe me or not, but my mom laughs right away.

"Oh honestly, Tammy. Your sister's the jokester." She looks over at my dad. "Isn't she funny?"

"I'm hoping that's what that was," he says, still not sure. After all, he did raise four girls, and we did have our share of fender benders.

I smile, and relief crosses his face.

"Harry. I can't believe you fell for that. You know as well as I do that if Tammy put any marks on your truck, she wouldn't bring it back until it was fixed. She's the responsible one, remember?"

Mom always did give us labels. They are good labels, I guess, but labels nonetheless. I'm the responsible one; Kori, my youngest sister, is the happy one, and sometimes Mom calls her Little Miss Sunshine.

That was never me. I guess I always did have a tendency to be more reserved.

And responsible.

Read: boring.

Not that Mom would ever say that. That's just what I hear when people say I'm the responsible one.

"I dished you out some ice cream, but I stuck it in the refrigerator so it wouldn't melt so fast. Go ahead and sit down, and I'll grab it."

I don't really want ice cream, but it looks like they are eating mint chocolate chip, which is one of my favorites, like a person could ever actually choose a favorite flavor of ice cream. As long as it doesn't have coffee in it. Still, ice cream is ice cream, cold and sweet, the perfect food.

I sit down on Dad's right side across the table from where Mom is sitting.

"Did you get everything okay?" Dad asks. I didn't tell him what I was doing. I knew he would probably try to talk me out of it.

"I did. Thanks." I want to try to change the subject before Mom joins the conversation. She won't hesitate to ask what I did.

But considering she's in the kitchen and has just shut the refrigerator door, my hope is a little far-fetched.

"What did you say you did with it again?" she asks as she sets my bowl full of ice cream down in front of me.

"I bought an ATV."

My mother had walked around the table and was in the process of sitting down. She freezes with her butt halfway to the chair.

"You what?"

My dad holds a spoonful of ice cream halfway to his mouth. "You bought a four-wheeler?" he asks, his tone nothing but disbelief.

I nod, trying to be casual, but their reactions aren't helping me. I have even less confidence now.

What was I thinking?

"I did. It's sitting at my house if you want to come see it." I take my spoon and scoop out a bit of ice cream. "It's a really pretty blue."

"Oh. Blue?" My mom says, her tone odd. "So, you bought it for a yard decoration?" she adds uncertainly.

"I think blue would look nice with her house. Yellow and blue look nice together," my dad says, sounding even more uncertain than my mom.

I want to laugh. My parents, the people who know me best in the world, are so sure that me and an ATV don't go together that they would guess that I bought it for a yard decoration before they would guess that I bought it to actually ride it.

This conversation is not helping me.

"It's a pretty expensive yard decoration," I say before I put the ice cream in my mouth.

I haven't eaten much of anything since my divorce.

It's been long enough you'd think I'd get over it, but food just makes me sick.

He took the boys, and that was worse than the fighting.

Everyone's always feeding me, which probably doesn't help, but I know that they love me, and they're doing what they think is best for me, so I always go along with it.

But since I'm almost half a century old, my parents don't give me a hard time if I get up from the table and my bowl is not empty.

"How expensive?" Mom asks. "Maybe we should get one for our yard?"

I think that's my mom's idea of a joke.

"Maybe you should. Your house is white, you could get pretty much any color you wanted." Playing along is better than actually talking about it. If I procrastinate long enough, maybe we'll start talking about something else.

"So are you actually planning on riding it?" my dad says, cutting to the point.

"Yes. I'm going on a charity run two weeks from Saturday." Silently, I thank Mr. Gabriel. Justin. I thank Justin.

"A charity run? Like up on the mountain?" Even though he's a vet, the animals' owners come in with them of course, and he's usually up on all the latest.

Of course he knows what a charity run is.

I nod. "Yep." Even though I have no idea. Is it on the mountain? I guess.

"You better be careful. Several times the fire company has been called to those things," my mom says. Then she lowers her voice. "Most of the time, the people were drunk."

I nod and try not to let my shock show on my face.

I guess asked Mr. Gabriel why I hadn't seen him in church when I'd asked him why I hadn't seen him around town.

He'd seemed confused and rightfully so, I suppose. Good Grief isn't exactly a hotbed of the social scene.

Still, riding around with people who are drunk doesn't exactly sound safe to me.

I committed though, and I would do what I said.

One time can't hurt me, and it will be good for me. If I am going to buy an ATV, I should learn to drive it.

"So, Mom," I start. "You always talked about your dad having a midlife crisis and leaving your mom when you were younger. I was wondering today...how old he was when that happened." I know this is an obvious question, but Mom always loves talking about her younger years, and I think I might get away with it.

"Oh, I don't know," Mom says, tapping her empty spoon against her chin before she grabs more ice cream with it. "I think he was about forty-six or forty-seven. We were all teenagers, except my oldest two brothers were out of the house. Yeah, forty-six."

Great. I beat my grandfather by one year.

"Why?" Mom asks.

"I was just wondering."

My dad speaks up. "People don't have to have a midlife crisis. It's not something that everyone goes through. I think when people aren't very happy with their lives, they look back on them and see all the things they could have done and decide that they need to hurry up and get started doing all the things they think they've missed." He raises his brows and looks at Mom as she nods at what he is saying.

"I feel like if you live your life right the first time, you're not going to look back and regret a bunch of stuff. That will cut out the need for most midlife crises."

I don't look up from my ice cream, but I'm not eating it either.

I look back on my life and see almost nothing but regret. There have been very few decisions that I've made that I am happy with.

Maybe this *is* a midlife crisis.

At least I hadn't walked out on my wife and seven children.

Like my grandpa did.

My ex already did that—only he just walked out on me.

I push away from the table. "Thanks so much for the ice cream."

Worry has entered my mother's eyes. Worry that's been there for years. I wish I can make it go away. I wish I could do something to fix it, but my stomach is knotted, and I can't eat any more if I tried.

She doesn't say anything about the ice cream. Instead, she smiles, but I can tell it's forced. "Thanks again for stopping in, honey."

She pushes back from the table and comes around and hugs me.

Dad stands up and hugs me too.

I can't even blame my parents. They, along with my sisters, are the one good thing in my life.

"I'll see you guys Sunday if not before," I say as I walk out.

"Sure will," Dad says as the door closes behind me.

Chapter 8

Tammy

"I want everyone to read from page two hundred twelve to two hundred twenty-five and answer the questions at the bottom of page two hundred twenty-six."

I stand in front of my class and write on the whiteboard while I'm talking to them. I'll also post the assignment on the class website.

But from experience, I know that there is a percentage of the class that won't do the homework. I want to give them every opportunity possible.

I turn back around. "Does anyone have any questions?"

They all look bored and ready for class to be over.

I love the subjects I teach, and in some classes, I get a lot of participation and interest.

It's funny how even just one student can change the entire dynamic of a classroom.

This class is one I've fought with all year, using every trick I've learned as a teacher, trying to get them excited about literature and writing and, yes, even grammar.

I'm one of those weird people who actually love to diagram sentences.

There's just nothing so satisfying about having a line for every word and every word on its line.

I understand that not everybody shares my enthusiasm, but I try. When you love something, I think it's human nature to want the rest of the world to love it too.

"We have about five minutes until the bell rings. You can begin on your homework now." I look over the class and then to the student who is sitting in the front row, right in front of me. By design. I moved him there about the second day of school back in September.

"Roy? Would you please come up to my desk?"

He doesn't look up, and he certainly doesn't look surprised.

He is probably expecting it. I've spent a lot of time talking to him this year.

This is frustrating to me because I know the kid is super-smart.

I just haven't been able to figure out how to tap into his interest, to make him want to apply his intelligence to the work I assign.

Writing seems to be extra hard for him.

I know, from experience again, some kids who are extremely intelligent have trouble translating what's in their brain to their fingers.

It's like the wiring connecting the two is messed up or something.

I've seen it over and over again, and I've been able to correct it in various degrees every time I've seen it.

Except with Roy.

But more than his wiring being messed up, his attitude is really what's holding him back.

He stands in front of my desk, his head down, his hair longish and hanging in his eyes.

Maybe this makes me an exception, but my particularly favorite students are the ones who have problems.

Maybe it's because I love the challenge.

Or maybe it's just because I love pulling for the underdog.

It's mostly because I feel like I can relate. School was never hard for me, but life sure has been.

"How's your rewrite coming, Roy?" I ask in a soft voice meant for his ears only.

I am not unaware of some of the scandals that have rocked other districts and teachers, and as much as I might like to come around and put my hand on his shoulder and truly look into his eyes, I stay in my chair and keep my desk between us.

"Haven't started it."

His answer doesn't surprise me, said in that voice that is not quite a man's voice but is not a little boy's voice anymore, either.

I sigh inside, but I don't allow my dismay to show on my face. "I'm sorry to hear that. I was excited that I was going to get to read about the Alaskan gold rush and panning for gold in the Yukon. I thought you said you were interested in that, too, which is why we changed the subject of your term paper."

He hasn't turned in a term paper. Originally, he'd chosen to write about Shakespeare, though I'm not sure why.

Regardless, with all the snow that we had this winter, we've missed a lot of school. It is now March, and he still hasn't turned in a term paper.

I hate to fail him, but if he doesn't help me out a little, I am going to have to.

I do have one more thing I could try, which I've only done a handful of times in my teaching career.

He hadn't made any comment after my last statement, so I speak again. "I'm coming out to see your parent tonight. School records indicate you live with your father. Is that correct?" I know my tone sounds formal. The idea of visiting his father makes me nervous.

Roy's dad didn't show up for parent-teacher conferences at the beginning of the year, but that isn't completely surprising. Only about a third of the parents did. And hardly any of the senior-high parents.

Typically, by the time their kids are that old, they have a pretty good handle on the parenting thing.

But Roy just moved in, less than a year ago, and I don't know his parents since they weren't from Good Grief.

"He works. He won't be there."

"He works all evening?"

"Until eight. We're open late on Thursday night. He works until closing."

"I see. Will you be home?" I ask, although I have no intention of going to see him without his father present.

"No. The bus drops me off at my dad's work, and I work there until closing."

I digest this information, wondering what kind of business his dad works at that allows a child to hang out for four or five hours after school.

"Would it be better for me to drop by your dad's work?"

"No," he says with a sullen tone that irritates me. As much as it makes me sad.

"All right then. I'll be at your house at eight thirty this evening. You can let your dad know to expect me."

"He's not going to want to talk to you," Roy says, peeking through his bangs and giving me the impression that what he's saying isn't true.

Most of the time when I visit parents, they claim to have no clue that their child is struggling or that I have spoken to them multiple times and continuously tried to help them improve.

I'm guessing Roy isn't any different. I suppose I'll see tonight.

I'm also not unaware, that sometimes parents lie to me.

Short of calling them on it, which I have never done, I simply have to accept their word.

It makes me sad, but some parents seem to care so little about their child's education that they won't bestir themselves enough to give them a hand.

This seems to be the case with Roy, but I will try to withhold judgment until I visit his dad this evening.

"My conscience won't let me rest unless I try." My tone softens, and I try to meet his eyes under the hair that's hanging down in front of them. "You have so much potential, and you're so intelligent. I want to see you rock this thing. Truly. I know you can. And I will celebrate when you do. But I can't do it for you." I end my little speech on a down note. I don't know if he's listening or not. I wish I could do an *A Christmas Carol* thing—take him by the hand and show him his future.

Without exception, every child that I've ever had that has come back to me, or that I've seen somewhere, will say, *I wish I would have listened to you.*

I've never had even one say, *I'm glad I didn't.*

Regardless, sometimes there are just kids I can't reach. I don't want Roy to be one of them. So I will go to his house and speak to his father, even if the idea scares me.

The bell rings, and Roy shifts his head enough that his hair falls to the side and he's able to look at me with at least one eyeball, questioning as to whether he can leave.

I want to keep him. I want to keep talking to him until he gets what I'm saying, understands it, and realizes that I'm not the enemy.

That I'm sincerely trying to help him.

But I give him a small smile and nod, and he turns and practically runs out the door, almost knocking one of his classmates down in the process.

The rest of the day goes by quickly; my favorite classes this year are at the end of my day, which gives me a lift.

I spend the time between the end of school and leaving for Roy's father's house, which my GPS tells me will take twenty minutes, grading papers.

Unlike a math teacher, who just has to make sure that the right letters and numbers are on the paper, I actually have to read and understand most of the homework I correct.

As well as the tests.

Grammar homework and tests, of course, are the easiest to grade.

I do know sometimes English teachers don't assign many writing assignments because of the time-consuming process it is to grade them.

I love writing. I love putting sentences together. I love twisting words and finding the perfect word. I love words. I love it all, and I want my kids to love it too.

Therefore, I assign a *lot* of writing assignments.

Reading is the best way to improve a child's writing.

And since practice makes perfect, writing is the next best way.

My classes can expect to do a lot of each.

I'm about three quarters of the way through the stack of papers that I needed to finish before it's time for me to leave.

I forget to check what Roy's father's name is. If I recall correctly, Roy has a different last name than his dad. Which is unfortunately all too common.

I realize this as I'm grabbing my purse and walking out the door, phone in hand with the address pulled up.

I take a split second to decide whether I want to be late, or whether I want to know his name when I'm standing on his doorstep.

I hate being late.

So I walk out.

I eyeball the four-wheeler that is still sitting in my yard exactly where Mr. Gabriel parked it the day before yesterday when he pulled it off my dad's truck.

I did take the key out, and it's hanging on the hook next to my house key inside the back door.

I'm busy on Saturday, but maybe after church on Sunday, I'll sit on it.

Maybe I'll start it.

I probably won't attempt to ride it.

What was I thinking?

It still seems crazy, but I'm also kind of proud of myself for doing something that I never thought I would do. And yes, I'm not ready to ride it yet or even start it, but maybe if I spend a couple of nights just going out and sitting on it, I feel like maybe I can putter across my small yard and, goodness, I'm not sure what I'll do when I get to the end of it.

Going forward seems like a big enough challenge. Backing up? I'm not sure.

Regardless, that's a problem I'll think about over the weekend. Not now.

However, I'm wondering if I might have somebody to talk to. Roy's father seems to have some knowledge of four-wheelers, considering that when I pull into his house, which appears to be a well-kept, one-story rambler that is not fancy but does have its own yard, I can see two four-wheelers parked in a shed at the end of the driveway.

Helmets are hooked on the handlebars. I realize I never purchased a helmet.

I'm not sure if Idaho has helmet laws. I will wear one anyway, of course.

Maybe if Mr. Gabriel actually comes to the basketball game, I'll ask him. I'm sure his store sells helmets. I remember seeing a wall with helmets hanging on it and thinking about it, but I guess my brain was concerned about other things and I forgot.

There is one pickup parked beside the house, and it looks a little familiar.

As I slam the door to my compact SUV and walk by it, I give it a second glance.

Did I see it in the parking lot of the four-wheeler store?

It seems kind of distinctive, in a manly-man kind of way, and definitely not the kind of pickup that I would give a second glance to normally, but it does seem a little familiar.

I have no knowledge of what men do with their pickups, and I mentally shrug, thinking that maybe several pickups in the area look similar to this one.

I don't know.

I head up the walk and note that the yard, which still has spots of snow in it, is free of garbage and other debris.

I've been on some pretty interesting properties the few times I've visited students.

This doesn't exactly scream wealth and prestige, but it doesn't scream negligence either. In fact, it says the opposite of negligence.

I'm thinking about this as I step up on the porch and knock on the door.

Maybe that's the reason I'm caught with my mouth open and all I can do is blink when the door opens and Mr. Gabriel stands in front of me.

The only consolation I can think of is that he looks just as shocked as I feel.

Chapter 9

Justin

The elegant lady is on my doorstep.

Tammy.

Tamera actually suits her better. At least, the way she looks now.

Buttoned up all prim and proper like an old-fashioned schoolmarm.

I'm surprised but not unhappy.

Funny. One meeting with a person and a little bit of conversation, and all I can think about all day is her.

I'm not going to miss the ball game tomorrow.

This is a sweet surprise.

All I can think to say is, "You missed me, didn't you?"

Maybe my voice comes out a little deeper, a little huskier, and there's definitely some tease in there.

I think, if she weren't so shocked, she would smile at that.

But either she's at the wrong house, or I am not the person she expected to answer the door.

I think I'm hoping for the first.

Unfortunately, her first words confirm the second.

"Are you Roy's father?" From her tone, I assume she's hoping I'm not.

"I am."

I'm not sure what Tammy has to do with Roy, but I know it's not gonna change my infatuation with her.

It's probably not going to change my attraction to her, either.

I open the door wider. "Why don't you come in and tell me about what you want?"

I half expect her to refuse, so I'm more than a little surprised when she does that lifted brow thing she does really well and steps into my house.

"Would you like to sit in the kitchen? I'll get you a cup of coffee. Or we can sit down in the living room. There might be a little dog hair on the sofa." I add this last bit partly because I'm embarrassed and partly because sometimes people are allergic to dogs.

Rex is my collie mix, but while his hair is currently on my sofa, he's out with Roy, who for some odd reason wanted to take a walk after we got home from work tonight.

I didn't have any supper ready, so I let him go.

Now, as Tammy murmurs that she'd take some coffee and I lead her to the kitchen, I think that maybe my son's absence might be planned.

I also just have an inkling that maybe Tammy looks like a school-marm because she *is* a schoolmarm. Did she mention something to that effect?

I start to feel a little unease and am happy to busy myself with the coffee maker after pointing out a chair for Tammy.

Not that I'm scared. I'm not.

But I have been taking my son's word for it that he's been doing his schoolwork. This new business venture, along with keeping everything else that I do running smoothly, has taken up a lot of my free time.

I haven't been as diligent as what I was when he first came.

But the kid is brilliant, like his mom, not me, and I don't worry too much about schoolwork.

I think I'm about to find out that I should have been more concerned.

"I'm sure Roy told you that I would be visiting you this evening," Tammy starts out, sounding anything but sure.

"Is that the line you always start with when you're pretty sure the parents have no clue that the teacher was gonna pay them a visit?" I ask, figuring I might as well be straight-up honest.

I suppose I have a few imperfections that I would rather stay hidden, but lying isn't my thing.

I hate being lied to, and that do unto others thing was drilled into me when I was a kid. I have never shaken it.

Honestly, I don't want to. Seems like really good advice.

She looks a little abashed as she settles herself in her chair, her back straight, her hands folded neatly in her lap while her legs are primly crossed.

I really want to sit and just look at that picture. For some reason, it strikes me in all the right places, maybe the way a beautiful painting might inspire someone to want to just stand and stare at it.

I am cognizant, though, that as a man, I'm not allowed to stare, so I don't.

That doesn't change the fact that I want to.

The thought kind of flashes through my mind that it would be nice to have permission to be able to just look at her. I guess in my experience, married couples don't usually sit and stare at each other, so maybe that urge would go away, but I kinda doubt it.

Isn't that why people put artwork up on their walls? Because they never get tired of looking at it? Because they want to have it right where they can see it and stare at it any time they want? Because it's interesting to them or gives them a good feeling?

That's part of the reason I love going backpacking. Idaho has tons of places that have absolutely spectacular views, and I've never gotten tired of sitting at the top of the hill and watching the sun come up over the horizon.

For about an hour beforehand, the sky is just ever changing and totally awe-inspiring.

I feel like I could look at Tammy the way I look at the morning sky. And never tire of it.

"You have me figured out, Mr. Gabriel. There are lots of families whose last names are not the same."

"If you knew my last name wasn't the same, didn't you recognize it?"

"I admit, when I walked out the door of my house, I remembered I'd forgotten to check and see what your name was. But I didn't want to be late."

Her voice is refined and cool. The casual sweater- and jeans-wearing woman of two nights ago is gone. Replaced by the woman who showed up in my shop.

I like them both, but I like the sweater-and-jeans woman better. I think there's even more underneath those layers. It interests me that she has so much depth to her personality.

It makes me feel like she's hiding something.

Or protecting something.

"I can't imagine you'd ever be late for anything," I say as I pour water into my coffee maker.

"I try to set the example that I expect for my students. Of which Roy is one. And from your comment, I assume he hasn't told you that he's been struggling in my English class this year."

"I've seen his grades haven't been the best, and we've talked about it some. But he's assured me that he's been doing the work. I've never had a problem with him before, and so I believed him." I fold my arms over my chest and lean against the back of the counter in front of the coffeepot, looking at her.

I'm aware that having my arms folded in front of my chest is a defensive position, and yet it feels like the most comfortable position, so I don't readjust.

I do however feel like she needs some background information on my son.

"I'm not Roy's biological father. My ex-wife had him from a previous relationship before she and I got together and eventually married. I adopted him. When she divorced me, she insisted on custody, and I didn't fight her. However, she always allowed me visits with my son."

The coffeepot hums, sounding familiar, as Tammy listens with her eyes never moving from my face.

I continue. "Roy was okay with the next man she married, but through that divorce, he spent more time with me, and then when the man she's currently living with came into the household, Roy asked to move in with me."

I shrug, the whole thing sounding sordid even to my ears. But it is the truth, and there is no point sugarcoating it.

"She allowed him to. Maybe because she was pregnant. I don't know. She's a good bit younger than I am, and it seems like she's starting a new family with this guy."

If Tammy is interested in any more details about my ex and my relationship, she doesn't ask. She is here to talk about my son, and she stays on the subject.

"So did Roy move in with you about the time you moved into the Good Grief school district?"

"He was with me for two and a half years before we moved, and he started ninth grade in Good Grief. It's been a hard couple of years for him, with no permanence and a lot of drama. I also suspect there might be reasons why he wanted to move out of my ex's home other than a personality conflict with her latest flame, but I asked around a little bit, and he didn't seem inclined to talk about it, and I didn't push him."

I'm down for communicating with my son, and even though heart-to-hearts might make me nervous, I'll do it if I need to.

Sitting down and talking about feelings isn't exactly my forte, and I don't push him where he doesn't seem to want to go.

"I see. That does explain a lot. I believe maybe he was a little over-whelmed in my class. And maybe he just shut down?" She lifts her brows a little and looks at me as though I might have the answer to what apparently was a question.

"Maybe." I have no idea what I'm supposed to say. I saw he had some lower grades than he'd ever brought home. I asked him if there were any problems. He said no. I told him he needed to do better or we'd get help for him. He said he would, and his past record indicated that he was a good student, so I didn't pursue the situation.

She is still looking at me, and while I want to just sit and listen to the coffee drip into the carafe, I speak. "I wasn't jumping on him, because I knew he'd been having a hard time adjusting to a new school and being in senior high. The D he brought home for the second quarter wasn't acceptable, but we talked about it, and he told me that he would do better and didn't need help. I haven't seen the third-quarter report, but if that D had become an F, I guarantee you that you and I would have been speaking at that point, because I instigated it, not you."

I have one foot crossed over the other as I lean against the counter. As much as I want to shake my foot or fidget in some way, I don't.

She's doing her job, and I admire that.

Also, just judging by the look on her face and also judging by the fact that she came to see me when she clearly didn't want to come, I know that she truly cares about my kid.

I can admire someone who does their job with their heart and not just their head and hands.

I like that.

I really don't need to see anything more about Tammy to inspire me to like her more than I already do.

I feel like I'm getting into some dangerous territory, and I want to back off.

Somehow.

But I can't figure that out and focus on the conversation, so I tuck that away to think about later.

Chapter 10

Justin

"I'm glad to hear you're concerned. Normally, when I get to the point where I feel like I need to make a visit to a parent, I find that they truly don't really care about their child's education. I'm glad that you are not the typical parent." Tammy's tone and facial expression all say she isn't completely convinced of the words she is saying.

I figure I better make sure she understands where I stand. "I'm not expecting my son to be an English major. I'm not even convinced that the stuff he's doing in your class is necessary for the direction he's heading in his life." She opens her mouth, but I put my hand up. "But I believe that when a man does a job, whatever he does, he needs to do it to the best of his ability. Whatever it is."

"Whatsoever thy hand findeth to do, do with thy might," Tammy murmurs, and I recognized it as a Bible verse, although I can't place it.

I nod my head.

Normally, I don't have a problem staying on the subject. But I feel like maybe I need to correct an impression that she might have gotten from when we've spoken before.

"There's a little church just about five miles down the road from here. When I first moved in, before I'd even gotten unpacked, even before the first Sunday had rolled around, the pastor from that church and one of his deacons visited me. I've been going there since I landed here. That's why you've not seen me in Good Grief on Sunday morning."

Yeah, just like I thought, the light dawns all over her face as she understands and realizes where I've been.

I know it's not a judgment. It's a desire to seek after someone who shares your values and beliefs. There's nothing wrong with that because it's not a discrimination against people who disagree with you; it's not even a statement that way. It's just nice to know you're in the presence of someone who doesn't just do things the way you do but understands you, too.

It's a natural human inclination, and there's no need to vilify it. I don't judge her for it.

I totally understand where she was coming from, and I understand the expression on her face.

She doesn't have to say anything, but she does.

"I've heard about that church. It's a good one." That's all she says, but it's enough.

I nod, not needing to say anything more.

I take a breath and turn toward the coffee, which is done.

I carry it and two cups over and set them down on the table in front of Tammy.

As I pour, I say, "Cream or sugar?"

"Cream, please," she says, and I get the feeling that she almost wants to get up to get it, but she doesn't.

While she looks very collected, as I'm standing close to her, I can sense more than see her nervousness.

In a way, it makes me admire her even more, that she's sitting here at my table, bluffing rather than show her fear.

I get the sugar canister out of the cupboard. I don't have any fancy serving bowls, so I set it along with the spoon in front of her before I go to the refrigerator and get the milk.

That's my cream.

It probably isn't going to meet her standards, but I know her well enough by now that I'm sure she won't complain.

I set it down, and then I sit down in the chair diagonally across from her. "So what do you suggest we do? About Roy?"

I do want to sit and talk to her, and I do want to talk about things other than Roy, but that's what she's come for, and I want to do that first.

I'm certain I like her, but I'm not certain how she feels about me. Those layers are making it hard.

That and the fact that I've spent more time staring at the sunrise than I have thinking about how to figure out women.

This is the first time in my life I've ever felt like I might have wasted my time.

"I'm willing to work with him, but I don't have time in class. It would either have to be after school or at my house or yours in the evening."

"You don't think he'll get caught up on his own?"

"I assigned a term paper that was due January thirty-first. He didn't turn anything in. Because I've done this before and I know that he has the intelligence to pull this off, to complete this assignment, I gave him a grace period. Because of all the snow days we had, I've extended his grace. But..." She shakes her head, and her eyes are sad. I don't have any trouble reading her expression and knowing that it pains her to have to fail a child who is capable of doing the work. "I can't give him a non-failing grade when he hasn't even turned anything in. This is a huge part of their third-quarter grade. He needs to do at least something."

"Term paper. How many pages? Is that how you assigned it?" I remember him saying that he flunked that paper and had a chance to rewrite it, but he didn't say that he failed it because he hadn't turned anything in at all.

"Three to five pages. Completely doable, especially for a kid with Roy's abilities."

"I'm just gonna say English was never my strong suit either. But I'll help him as much as I can." I stir my coffee and watch it swirl. "He's not having any trouble with the grammar and the other parts of your class? It's just the term paper?"

She nods. "I don't think he studies for the tests, but he gets solid Cs. If he applied himself, he would be a straight-A student."

"I believe that. That's what his grades have always been." When he was with me anyway. My ex wasn't exactly the greatest communicator. Well, she didn't have a problem talking. She just didn't typically talk to me.

And, in the interest of fairness, I never call her unless I need to talk about Roy. I haven't talked to her about this problem, either.

So there. I can complain about my ex, but the fault is mostly with me.

"So he needs help, especially for this term paper, to get him a passing grade for the third quarter. How soon does he need to turn it in?"

"Two weeks at the very latest. And that means that I will turn his grade in late," Tammy says, looking me straight in the eye.

"Okay."

"I have everything I need, but when I go to write, everything's a jumble."

I hadn't heard Roy walk in. My head whips around. I go back through the things that Tammy and I have said.

I don't know how long he's been there, but I don't think he heard anything that I wouldn't have wanted him to hear.

Both of us are saying he can do it. I don't want him to blame any inability of his to do his work on anything other than himself. I hope he didn't hear me mention the instability in his life.

That is all true, but that's life.

I feel it's far better to teach a child that whatever happens to him, he's still responsible for his responses and for doing what he is expected to do.

Personal responsibility. I want my kid to own it.

I know Tammy is surprised to see Roy in the doorway, but just as I'm wondering how to approach this with him, Rex must have realized that we have a guest, and he shoves past Roy, his tail going a hundred miles an hour, and he pushes into Tammy.

Tammy hasn't struck me as a dog person, far from it. So I'm kind of surprised when she smiles at Rex and scratches his ears.

Rex of course is dancing around, trying to figure out how he can get his nose into her mouth or next to her nose at the very least, and I am afraid he's going to forget his manners.

"Stay down, Rex," I say, not raising my voice at all, because Rex is a smart dog. He's part border collie and part unknown, and he understands voice commands.

That was something that Roy and I did when he came to visit me when he was younger. We spent a lot of time training Rex.

We spent a lot of time in the woods too.

My eyes slip to Tammy again, and I wonder if maybe that's part of her layers.

This dog thing, where she's petting Rex and not backing away from him. Not scared and not trying to keep herself clean. It's a layer I wasn't expecting.

Maybe there's another layer under there, a backpacking, outdoorsy, loves to watch the sunrise from an uninhabited ridge layer in there.

I hope.

Holy man, I hope.

"How about you come in and sit down, son. We're talking about what we're going to do about this term paper that you haven't done."

"I told you. I have all the information I need, but when I go to write it, I can't get it out past the jumble in my head."

Tammy has been whispering sweet words of adoration to my dog.

I'm not jealous.

Okay. I'm a little jealous.

So I don't think she's listening, but she looks up and says, "You know, Roy, you might not believe this, but that's a common problem. Two easy things will help right off. One is learning to type. And the other thing is after getting someone to help you organize your information, you say a sentence out loud before you write it down."

My brow shoots up.

Those are commonsense suggestions, and they should work. I hadn't considered typing instruction. He should have gotten that somewhere in his education. But I guess moving around from school to school, it had gotten missed.

It's so much easier to get my thoughts down when I type, because it's faster.

Tammy gives Rex one last pat on his head. My dog has fallen so completely in love with the woman that I've got my own eye on he doesn't even come greet me. Instead, he turns around one time and lays down at Tammy's feet.

Her feet are long like her fingers, and I bet they're slender too, but I can't see. Not that I would stick my head under the table and look exactly, but it annoys me just a little that Rex gets to lie on top of them.

Tammy, in the meantime, has started up a conversation with my son after giving him that advice. She's offered to have him at her house or come here and help him organize his information, and she's giving more specifics on getting the words from his brain out his fingers.

She's also offered to see if she can get him out of his fourth-period study hall and into a typing class, even if it's given by an older student who simply helps him work through the beginning typing book.

Roy doesn't look super thrilled, but he looks a lot less belligerent than he did when he had been standing in the doorway.

He has that tall, gangly, awkward movement and the voice that is half boy, half man, and I remember those days all too well myself, even if I'm going on half a century.

Of course, I remember them with fondness, because back then I didn't wake up with pain in my back, or the belly that has somehow grown over my belt loop overnight, or hair that is thinning, or ears that don't hear nearly as well as they used to, or streaks of gray in the hair that is left, or a whole world of regrets as I get out of bed alone.

I don't typically dwell in the past. There is no point. But it is hard not to look at my son and think about things I could have done differently and about the mistakes I don't want him to make.

I guess they really don't need me, because I don't say anything while Roy and Tammy talk. Actually, it's Mrs. Fry to Roy, which interests me, because obviously she's not wearing a ring, but she's a missus.

They make plans for her to come out here and help him.

I kind of miss the bulk of their conversation, but I think I understand that my son is going to be giving her lessons on how to ride her four-wheeler.

We have forty acres here and a nice mountain trail, short, not too steep, and definitely not challenging. Just a nice place to ride.

He's offered it to her.

I smile.

I didn't have to try to figure out how to spend more time with Tammy. She's going to be at my house.

But not tomorrow, because there's a ball game, and not the next day, because she's doing something with the fire station, and not Sunday morning, because she's going to church.

Sunday afternoon. I'll see her again Sunday afternoon, unless...unless I change churches.

Unless...unless I go to the fire hall and participate in whatever activity is happening there, which I have no clue.

I think I like the idea of "unlesses," and I plan on implementing them.

Chapter 11

Tammy

I walk into the gym. Early of course. All the girls are warming up.

I have my bag with me and a whole stack of papers that need to be graded.

I typically try to sit by myself and grade papers every spare second.

It's the life of the teacher.

Especially an English teacher.

I've heard that other school districts have gone to an electronic system where kids even do their schoolwork online.

I suppose, at some point, Good Grief will get with the program, but I'm not sure how I feel about it.

Of course, no one likes change, and it always seems to make things harder before they become easier, but I know it's good for kids to have something to hold in their hand, to see and touch.

Computer screens just aren't the same.

But maybe that's me being old-fashioned.

Hard to imagine I've gotten to the point where I'm old-fashioned.

But it does drive home the point I'm old.

I'm probably too old to be thinking about romance.

I know all ages of people do. Even people in the assisted living center, where my sister Leah works, have romances.

Still, I know I'm not fresh and pretty the way I used to be. My back hurts, my knees hurt depending on the weather, I can't eat what I used to, can't do what I used to, and I feel like I have scars all over my insides.

It's hard to imagine that someone would want me.

I know. Self-esteem and all that.

I've never really bought into self-esteem. It feels like an imaginary thing to me, where you make yourself out to be better than what you are.

Maybe it has to do with positive thinking. I don't know.

Regardless, those are just the facts.

It used to be, when my sister Claire first started coaching the girls' team, I could sit wherever I wanted to, because the stands were pretty much empty. But since Trey Haywood moved back and became her co-coach, things have changed.

There are actually a lot of people here tonight, and it will get more crowded.

I go up to the highest bleacher and sit at the top in the corner. It doesn't have the best view, and I'm more likely to not have company.

I love to watch my niece, Evie, play, and I love to watch my sister coach, and I'm here to support them and our high school in general.

After all, I'm a teacher here.

But I'm not that interested in basketball, and I'd rather focus on getting my papers graded. So, yes, I'm antisocial, and I sit down, figuring I have time to grade at least two more papers after glancing at the digital clock winding down.

I don't think Justin is coming. Mr. Gabriel, I correct myself.

All day long, I call teachers by their title and their last name. It's kind of a habit.

I don't think too much about it.

But I suppose it's also a way to stiff-arm. Like a protection thing. Whatever it is, I don't think too much about it; it's just something I do.

I have my nose down and my pen following along as I read a student's answer, explaining the problem between Romeo and Juliet in response to an essay question on a test I gave today.

I've just read, "The dude needed Snapchat, and then he wouldn't have had that problem," when I realize there's someone looking down at me.

I can't argue with the truth, but it wasn't exactly what I was going for by way of an answer, and I haven't figured out what to say, so I figure this is probably a good time to be interrupted.

My eyes fall off my paper and onto the boots that are beside me. They look familiar.

My heart recognizes them and is trying to jump out of my chest and shake hands.

I feel like I'm at a distinct disadvantage, as I have my feet propped on the bleacher seat in front of me, my papers in my lap, a pen in my hand and one behind my ear, because I always like to have a spare, and that seems like the best place to keep it, the least likely place for it to get lost, especially here where I've lost more than one pen under the bleachers.

Kids look at me awfully funny when I climb underneath to get it.

I only did that once.

Some things aren't worth sacrificing your dignity for.

"Hello," Mr. Gabriel says, and I'm pretty sure his eyes hook for more than a second on the pen behind my ear.

I'm tempted to reach up and grab it, but he's already seen it, so what's the point?

"Good evening, Mr. Gabriel," I say, pretending as hard as I can that I'm a dignified person, in a dignified position, which is anything but true, but at least my words are dignified.

"So is this seat taken?" he says as he nods beside me.

"It's not." I know right then that I'm probably not going to get any more papers corrected.

Normally, this would make me a little bit sad, because I like to have test papers ready to hand back the next day, and in order to do that, I'll be up well past midnight.

But I can't deny I would rather talk to Mr. Gabriel than correct papers any day.

"You can call me Justin," he says, and there's some kind of seductive tone in his voice, nothing overt, just something that makes me look at him longer and with interest.

Am I hearing things?

"After all, I call you Tammy."

Right. Not that I'd given him permission to. But that was kind of old-fashioned anyway. No one needs anyone's permission to use their first name anymore.

I want to use his first name, but it seems like a breach of my defenses. I don't want to make a big deal about it though, because I don't want him to know that it makes me uncomfortable.

"That's fine," I say, and I'm proud of the total unconcern in my voice.

"Justin." He grins, as though knowing it is a stumbling block for me, and it feels like he's issued me a challenge.

So, I admit I like challenges.

What I guess I should say is I like to rise to the challenge.

"So, Justin." I say his name, the ceiling doesn't fall down on me, but I still feel a little tight in my chest and hope I'm hiding it well. "You decided to come to a basketball game."

"I said something to Roy, and he said he'd love to go." He sits down, putting one boot on the seat in front of us while his other leg rests perilously close to me. "We worked on his term paper today, by the way. I think he has a list of questions he's going to want to ask you on Sunday when he sees you. But I did the best I could."

"That's fine. I appreciate it. I'll be prepared for questions on Sunday afternoon."

"He's also looking forward to giving you a four-wheeler lesson."

I allow myself to smile a little and tell myself it's okay to loosen up just a bit. After all, I'm wearing jeans, although I didn't quite go the hooded sweatshirt route. I'm wearing a cardigan.

I look my age, I know.

Although I do have cute boots on. Not high-heeled boots or anything, I hardly ever wear heels, because I'm already tall enough, but cute for a size eleven.

All right. I'm wearing *nice* boots. Not cute. I don't think I have anything that's cute.

"I notice you didn't exactly jump for joy or say you're looking forward to your four-wheeler lesson."

I shake my head. I wasn't even thinking about four-wheelers. "Sorry. I actually got a little distracted thinking about my boots. I..." I can't lie. "I'm not looking forward to any four-wheeler lessons. In fact, where you parked it when you got it off my dad's truck is where it's still sitting."

"Seriously?" he said, his brows raised.

I nod. I've got to own it.

"That's crazy. Most of the time, people buy a four-wheeler, and they can't wait to run it. Have you even touched it?"

"I took the key out of it. Does that count?"

"No," he says with a chuckle, and I can tell from the look on his face he has no idea what to think of me.

I suppose that's better than not liking me?

I don't know. I don't want to care. I don't care at all.

Caring means letting defenses down and opening yourself up to hurt.

I don't want to go there.

"I don't know what you're thinking about, but it brought clouds to your face, and I don't like it," Justin says, and it surprises me, because he's not the kind of person that I would have thought would say something about "clouds" on someone's face. But it makes me think that he really did notice that I was kind of going in a bad direction in my head.

I look at him with a little more consideration than I had before. "Clouds?"

He grins. "How else do I say it? You were smiling, and I thought we were getting along okay, and then all the sudden, it's like..." His hand comes up, and it runs down over his face like a blind. "You change. You're not smiling and happy anymore. And I haven't said anything."

"Don't we all have things we think about that don't make us happy?" I ask, in a very casual tone. I'm not going deep with him.

I'm not going deep with anyone.

I was there for a long time, and I'm done.

"I guess we do." He seems to think a little bit, then he says, "I mean I do, but I don't think about them. You know?"

"I try not to. I guess sometimes we just like to torture ourselves, right?"

He shakes his head no. "No way. I'm not torturing myself if I don't have to. I definitely don't have to. Except..." The side of his mouth curves up in that half grin I'm starting to love. "When my son's English teacher comes around. I don't really want to have to work on writing a term paper, I thought I was done with that for the rest of my life, but I do it, torture myself, because I don't want her to be disappointed in me."

"She's more likely to be disappointed in your son, although she's not going to be disappointed in anyone. She's going to hope for the best, and expect it, and be satisfied with whatever he does, because whatever he does is so much better than what he has done which is nothing."

At that, the buzzer sounds, and we both look out toward the floor where the girls have put their balls away and gone over to the sidelines.

His eyes watch the girls as his body leans a little bit toward me, and he says out of the corner of his mouth, "My son calls you Mrs. Fry. That makes me think that you *were* married. I guess, if you *are* married, I should find somewhere else to sit."

I like it. I really, really like it. I like the fact that he's concerned about that and will do something about it.

Right now, I know of two affairs that are going on in the teacher faculty. People who don't care that someone else is married.

Sometimes even I want to justify those, because I know the one woman who's having an affair, with a much younger, very handsome, single male teacher, is in a terrible relationship, and I wouldn't want my worst enemy to be married to her husband.

But it doesn't make it right.

Not that I am judging them; I just always think about the kids.

A person makes a vow, and they intend to keep it, but when they don't, it's not just them that gets hurt.

I wish, I wish *so hard* that my husband had known that. That he knew it now.

That he cared. He'd been far more interested in making himself happy than he was in doing what was best for our boys.

Or me.

"There's that cloud again," Justin says casually.

"I'm sorry. You're right. I am Mrs. Fry, but I'm divorced." I hold out my hand where my wedding ring used to be. It's been off for years now, and there's no little white ring, no indentation, no sign that I wore a man's ring for years.

A ring is only a symbol. Taking it off doesn't actually end anything.

I'm not sure anything actually does end.

It just isn't physical anymore. But it feels like it's still in my head.

"I already told you I was. Not my choice. Hers," he said, and he moves his leg, propping his boot beside the first on the seat in front of us in a wide stance, and he leans his elbows on his knees.

That makes him uncomfortable.

"Clouds," I say.

He turns, with that half smile, and meets my eyes. "I deserve that."

"Not deserve. I was just acknowledging."

"Thanks. I didn't need you to tell me about it, I just want to make sure that I wasn't stepping into something that I was going to regret."

"He's been gone for years. It's been final almost that long. His girl-friend wanted to get married right away. She was pregnant." I stack my papers, tapping them on my lap to make sure that they are even on the bottom, although that is unnecessary, and I put them in my bag along with the pen in my hand and the one behind my ear.

That's all the more I am going to say about that.

Chapter 12

Justin

Obviously, she doesn't like the topic.

I can't blame her. I don't know anyone who enjoys talking about their divorce.

Seems like so many of us have them.

Even if I don't feel like the failure of my marriage is all my fault, it still feels like my failure.

And when I am being honest, I admit that I am at fault. At least half.

It is so easy to look back and blame everything on her.

I hope if I ever get a chance to do it again, although I am not sure I actually want a chance, I hope I have become a better person because of the lessons I've learned.

"You still love him," I say, and I can't look at her. I don't want to see the truth on her face.

She snorts. That does make me look, because Tamera Fry is not the snorting kind of woman.

But yeah, there's derision on her face. And I don't doubt it when she says, "No."

"He must have hurt you pretty bad."

That's not a comment I would typically make.

But I feel like I have to because it's obvious. There's a lot of emotion there. And I want to know her. It's kind of like when I'm sitting on that mountain, and I'm looking off at the sunrise. I want to see everything at once, and I don't want to miss a thing, because I know it'll never happen again. Never ever, not the way it's happening that morning. Sure, there'll be other sunrises, but never one like that.

Every second that you spend with your eyes on something else, you're missing something beautiful.

Maybe I'm the only one, but I can't ever see enough, can't have it last long enough. Sunrises don't last long.

I've compared her in my head to sunrises before, and that's what it feels like now.

I don't want to miss anything. I want to know it all.

"When he left, he took my boys. I never thought he'd actually get custody. I mean, come on, he missed their birthdays, he missed their doctors' appointments, he was never there to help me with anything, I raised them myself practically, and yet, he hired a lawyer, who said that I was cold and heartless and didn't care about my kids, and he got people to lie for him. I mean, they put their hand on the Bible, and they said things about me that were absolutely not true." She looked down. "I might have..." She swallows. " I might have lost it on the one witness..."

"Lost it?" I look at the cool and collected woman beside me. I can't imagine her losing anything, let alone her temper or whatever it was.

"They said they saw me at a bar with some guy they knew, and they brought in a man to say that he was with me. Who were these people? I didn't even know them." She sighs, her frustration obvious. "I couldn't prove that I didn't know him, and maybe, maybe if I could have sat there and taken it without flipping out because they were lying about me, maybe the judge wouldn't have ruled the way he did." She looked down, folding and unfolding her hands.

The ball game was about to start. The girls had been introduced, and they'd run out on the court.

I had skeletons in my own closet, but I could feel her pain that she lost her boys.

"And later, when they got older, when I tried to revisit custody, the judge asked them who they wanted to live with, and they both said their dad."

I think that was probably the thing that hurt her the most, although I could be wrong.

She said that with the least amount of emotion.

I don't want to marginalize what she told me, but I also don't want to dwell on it.

I let a few minutes go by, as play commences, and then I say, "Are you here just to support the high school, watch your sister coach or do you know someone who is playing?" I strive for a lighter, casual tone.

She looks relieved that I've changed the subject, and she almost smiles. "Number twenty-six? That's my niece."

"She has your height," I say easily. She's a cute little girl and the best ballplayer on the court.

"She's good."

I look over at Tammy and give her a once-over. "You play?"

Her cheeks get a little pink, and she shakes her head. Her lips turn up slightly, and I think I've charmed her.

Which is no small feat, considering I'm not a charming man and she is not an easy lady to charm.

I think the Lord must be on my side, and I silently thank him.

"You know my sister is coaching."

"Did you guys have the same parents?" I say, and I hope she hears the teasing in my voice. I don't mean anything by it, but the lady that she pointed out as her sister is shorter and curvier.

She laughs. "She got all the good genes in the family."

I want to grab a hold of her over that one. I turn, and maybe my words are a little harsher or more strong than I mean for them to be. "That's not true. That's not even close to being true. You're tall and slender, and you remind me of a painting or a beautiful sunset that a man can't take his eyes off of."

Yeah. Serves me right for spending so much time thinking about Tammy and sunsets and Tammy and paintings and now, stupidly, the words come out my lips. I certainly hadn't meant to say anything like that.

But she makes me angry. "I'm not calling your sister ugly. I'm just saying you've got good genes."

I don't even know what else to say. Boy, that was romantic. *You've got good genes.* No wonder I can count on one hand the number of dates I've had in the last ten years.

I blow out a breath. I'd rather have one date with the right woman than one hundred dates with wrong ones. But still, I like to be able to say the right thing when the right thing is necessary.

Her head turns toward me, and she's biting her lip. "Sunset?" she asks softly.

I nod. "I know. Not romantic. I'm sorry."

"It is. Thank you." She looks back at the game and claps as the girl she said is her niece makes a three-point shot. Good Grief is now ahead. "I'm not beautiful. I'm not falling for flattering words or anyone that tries to say I am, but I feel like you meant what you said. Thanks."

She doesn't look at me when she speaks, and it kinda makes me feel like maybe she had a hard time saying it. For whatever reason.

Maybe her husband never complimented her.

Or maybe he insulted her.

Or maybe it was somebody else. I don't know. I kinda want to find out, but I want to get back on solid ground.

I haven't known her long enough to talk in depth about these things.

"Your niece is pretty good," I say, wondering why I have such a hard time having a simple conversation with her. Casual.

No pain allowed.

"She is. And she loves to play. She's actually only thirteen."

That sets off warning bells in my head.

Part of the reason that Roy wanted to come to see the game was because he said there was a really good player on the team, and she was cute.

"Thirteen?" I say, hoping somehow that she said fifteen and I misheard.

"I know. She's tall. My sister always says she takes after her husband, but there are tall genes in the family." Tammy flattens her lips and kinda shrugs her shoulders like what can she do about it.

"I like those tall genes."

"I almost hate them. Most of the time. I know models are tall, and a lot of actresses, but in real life, it's tough in a lot of ways." Her lips turn up slightly. "Although one nice thing about being tall is you can be heavy but not show it, since your weight is distributed over a larger area."

"You don't have that problem," I say, and then I say, "Not that I've ever looked anywhere but your face." I say it kinda sarcastically, and she gets me, because her lips quirk even more.

I like that.

"But it is kind of a bummer, because pretty much three quarters of the male population is undatable, unless I want to go out with a guy who's shorter than I am."

"Nothing wrong with that. I date ladies who are shorter than me all the time." I let out half a breath. "Okay. That was a total exaggeration. I don't date all the time. I actually don't date much at all. But pretty much every date I've ever had is with a woman who is shorter than me. It's not that bad," I say, knowing that there is a difference and just teasing her.

She picks up on it immediately and shoots back, "It might be nice for you, but it stinks for me." She lifts that shoulder again, slender. Too slender, I think, and I wonder about that a little. "Men don't like feeling small next to me. Which is what happens. I don't like feeling like an Amazon woman and looking down on my date. My mom always said if I fell for a guy who was shorter than I was, she would know it was true love. I suppose that's true."

"So what if you fall for a guy who's taller than you?" I ask, because I am taller than her.

"What about it?"

"Doesn't your mom have anything wise to say about that?"

"I guess not. I never threw myself over her bed crying because there were boys in school taller than me. It was always because there were no boys in school taller than me."

"Oh. So it involved tears?"

She gives me a baleful glance.

"Hey, I'm just asking. You don't exactly look like the kind of woman who cries a lot."

"I wouldn't call myself that either."

The other side of the gym erupts in cheers as their point guard gets fouled on a layup and makes the basket anyway.

They line up for foul shots.

"So why did you ask about Evie?" Tammy asks, and I remember that she's perceptive.

"Well, this isn't something you can tell anyone, but there were two reasons Roy wanted to come tonight. The first was that he admitted to me that he played basketball in junior high back at his old school when he lived with his mom." I let out a breath. "I didn't know that and hadn't even mentioned basketball to him this year. Maybe that's a good thing, since he's been struggling with the schoolwork, and basketball would have taken his mind off it even more."

"That could be, or maybe it would have given him more motivation to buckle down and do it. I think that's all he needs. That and a little bit of help rewiring his brain," she says, keeping her eyes on the floor as Evie brings the ball down the court. "And what's the other thing?"

"I think he has a crush on Evie."

Chapter 13

Justin

Tammy's head snaps around, her brows drawn. "She's only thirteen."

"I'm not sure he knew that." I lift a shoulder. "I thought she was older."

Tammy nods her head. "Because I was tall, everyone always thought I was older too. I'm sure Evie gets that as well."

"That makes sense to me. Although I don't think it's applicable now," I say, solely to get brownie points, even though I also believe it.

She sees right through me. "You are totally trying to work me."

"Maybe. But I meant it."

Her eyes glint, and I almost think she might be flirting with me. "Did you?"

"I guarantee you I did. But...I was also trying to get brownie points." She keeps her eyes on the floor, but there's a smirk hovering around her lips. So I press. "Did I?"

She slants a glance at me, and her eyes narrow. "Maybe."

Definitely flirting. I like it.

"I'm all about the brownie points. Don't think I'm not going to keep trying," I say.

I'm tempted to slide just a little closer to her. There's probably six inches between us, and that's way too much.

"Feel free," she says, and there's definitely flirting in her tone.

The buzzer for the first quarter sounds, just as Evie fires off another three-point shot. The crowd roars when the ref indicates she shot after the buzzer.

"That's not the slightest bit true," I say. I just sat here and watched her. "The buzzer sounded just as the ball was going in the hoop."

"I agree. Every time that ref does one of our games, I feel like he roots for the other team. No matter who they are. I think he has something against Trey."

"That's the guy that's coaching with your sister?"

"Yes. He was an all-state baller when he was in school. I don't know the ref, at least I don't remember him, but maybe he was on a rival team or something."

"I suppose that's possible. Seems like an awful long time to hold a grudge, though."

"It could be something else. I've never actually talked to Claire about it."

I believe she's right. There's a problem somewhere, because now that I'm paying attention, that ref is definitely unfair. I can't believe they continue to get him.

Maybe they're short on refs.

It's not something we can do anything about, so I put it out of my mind. "I'll say something to Roy. I don't think he knew Evie's age, and I'm pretty sure it should make a difference."

"It has to. She's only thirteen, and I know she's not allowed to date."

"Of course not."

"The center, her name is Rachel, I think she's his age or maybe older, I don't know. But she's a nice girl from what I understand. She was good in class anyway."

"Maybe I can redirect him." I'm kinda thinking not though. I don't say that to Tammy, but I know I settle on one girl, and that's all I want. It happened with my ex, and it's happening for the second time in my life right now.

I suppose Roy isn't my flesh and blood, but it's crazy the things he does that are just like me.

I kinda hope this is one of them, because so many guys have wandering eyes, and they're never satisfied with the girl they've got.

Some women are like that too.

Not me. I get hooked on one, and that's all she wrote.

Unfortunately—maybe I shouldn't say unfortunately, but I slide a glance over to Tammy, whose eyes are glued on the ball game where her niece is bringing the ball down the court again—I'm definitely hooked. I don't even think she knows it.

Staying hooked on one girl isn't the problem, it's getting hooked on a girl who isn't hooked on me.

One of the other defenders sets a pick. Evie doesn't see it and plows straight into her. They both end up on the floor, and Tammy gasps.

"It's not supposed to be a contact sport," I say, looking at her, then looking back at Evie. "I think she's okay. She didn't hit her head."

"I know. And you're right, basketball is supposed be easy to watch, but twice now, I've seen girls hit the floor so hard it knocked them out. It scares me. I feel like they should wear helmets or something."

I laugh, but it could be coming. It wouldn't shock me. It would probably be safer, but sometimes, I think we overdo things.

All in all, I have a very enjoyable evening with Tammy, and I'm pretty sure she enjoys her time with me.

Maybe she'd rather have gotten her papers corrected, but she didn't act like it, and for the rest of the night, we manage to avoid talking about anything that might bring clouds to either of our faces.

After the game is over, with Good Grief winning by three points, I ask, "Can I walk you out?"

I know men aren't supposed to admit to nervousness, but getting those words out made my stomach twist in all kinds of crazy directions.

After all, she could tell me no.

"I guess. I suppose we're both going to the same place. Unless you parked your car somewhere other than the parking lot."

It wasn't exactly a "yes, I'd love to have you walk me out," but it was better than a "no."

She gathers her things, and I wait for her, my eyes sweeping the floor where the girls have already slapped hands and a couple of them are talking to friends and a few adults.

I see Roy. He's left the group of friends he was sitting with, and he's gone down to the bottom of the bleachers. I'm sure it is calculated on his part that he reaches the floor just as Evie is walking by.

He doesn't run into her, and I'm thankful for that, but I'm definitely not thrilled to see them talking.

I'm staring, and it doesn't take Tammy long to figure out what I'm staring at.

"I'll have to say something to her mother," she murmurs.

"You do that. I'll be talking to Roy."

She looks at me with gratitude in her eyes. I haven't even done anything, and I somehow feel proud. A look like that will do that to a man.

"Thanks."

It's on the tip of my tongue to say "anything for you," but I close my lips around the words.

She's barely agreed to walk out with me. I can't start saying stupid stuff like that.

I want to offer her my arm as we walk down the bleachers, but I've been told on more than one occasion by a woman that she can do it herself, and it makes me hesitate.

I was brought up that's a gentlemanly thing to do, but my life experience has told me that many women don't appreciate it.

And then I think to myself, do I want to be with a woman who doesn't appreciate a considerate gesture from a man and takes offense at it?

No one likes to be rebuffed, but I'd rather learn now than later when it might be too late.

"Let me help you," I say, holding out my hand.

She looks at it for a moment, then her hand comes up and slips in it.

My face doesn't smile, but my heart does.

"Thank you," she says.

My first wife was a lot younger than I was, but Tammy was brought up in the same generation as me.

I think we value the same things.

Some of the same things.

She doesn't ride four-wheelers, and I sell them.

Maybe we can rectify that.

I get to the floor and look over at my son. It's the kind of look that makes him feel like someone's looking at him. He glances up and meets my eyes.

I lift my brows and jerk my head, and he gets the memo. I see him typing into his phone as Evie speaks. My chest deflates.

He's getting her number.

She's giving it to him.

This could complicate things between Tammy and me. I don't want to be too hard on my son, but I feel like I need to nip this in the bud.

She's too young. And Tammy will not be very happy with me if anything happens between them, since I know about it.

But I want to tread carefully, because there's nothing that makes a man want to do something more than being told that he can't.

I debate about talking to Tammy about it, and I decide if she had seen something and not said anything to me, I would feel like she didn't trust me.

It's not that I don't trust her, it's just that I don't want to endanger anything that I might be building right now. I want more with her.

We push open the heavy doors at the side of the building that lead directly onto the parking lot. Many of the people who were watching the game are parents and are still waiting on their children. The parking lot isn't crowded.

"Where are you parked?" I ask.

She directs us to the left, which is the opposite direction of my pickup, and I lead her that way.

Sly guy that I am, I never let go of her hand when we came down from the bleachers. I'm holding it now. Her fingers are slender and long, and they feel just as good as I thought they would when I saw her signing her name.

I don't want to let her go.

Still, I have to say this. "I'm pretty sure my son just got Evie's number." My words fall out into the crisp night air.

It might be March, and almost spring, but spring comes slowly in Idaho.

"You think?" Tammy turns to me, concern stamped on her face.

"I'm pretty sure. She was talking, and he was typing on his phone. I suppose that could mean a couple of other things. Maybe he was getting her Snapchat handle or Facebook or whatever kids do now."

"I know it's hard to keep up. I'm around them every day, and every day, it feels like I get further and further behind. Evie's never been interested in anything but basketball. I don't even think she's ever looked at a boy. In fact, I'm not even sure she realizes there *are* such things as boys." She sighs. "She's so innocent in some ways. And so young."

"I know. I'm going to talk to him. Tonight."

I don't want to. I kind of dread it. But it actually could be for my son's protection. There's enough of an age gap between them that when he turns 18, he could be in trouble. If a relationship even lasted that long, which more than likely it wouldn't.

But, again, I kind of feel like Roy is the kind of boy that gets hooked and doesn't let go.

"I appreciate that. I'll call my sister tonight too. Hopefully, we can make sure that nothing inappropriate begins."

"Hopefully," I say, not sounding very hopeful.

"My car's right here," she says and tugs on my hand.

It is the kind of tug that says "come with me," not "let my hand go." Don't ask me how I can tell what the difference is. I just can. And trust me, I don't let go.

She unlocks her door with the key that she has in her hand. I didn't even realize she'd pulled it from somewhere.

I open her door for her. That is another thing that I was taught and something she appreciates if the look on her face is any indication.

"Thank you. I can't remember the last time someone opened my door."

"Now you can," I say. I don't have to tell her it is the way I was raised, what I believe, and what I did for my wife as long as we were married, no matter how she treated me.

This is just what a man does.

"Thank you for sitting with me. I enjoyed talking with you," she says as our hands slide apart, and she stands on one side of the door while I stay on the other.

I've thought about kissing her a lot. Not gonna lie. But I hadn't considered kissing her tonight.

Not that I would pass up the opportunity, but I'm sure she doesn't want to be kissing in the parking lot where her students might see her.

I'm disappointed. I can't help it.

But Tammy is more to me than just someone to kiss, and I say, "I wasn't sure whether I would enjoy watching a basketball game when I didn't know anyone. You made it fun. Thanks."

She smiles at the compliment, and I'm glad I said it.

"I'll see you Sunday afternoon," she says as she slips into her seat.

I don't say that I'm planning on seeing her sooner than that. But I am.

Chapter 14

Justin

Roy and I don't say much on the way home.

I do ask him questions occasionally, and he typically has never had a problem talking to me. Of course, the older he gets, the less he says, but I feel like that's normal.

I'm not sure how to broach the subject of Evie, and I decide I don't want to do it in the car.

When we get home, it's after eight o'clock. Later than we normally eat, except on Thursdays when I get home late.

"You want to help me fry some hamburgers?" I ask.

"Sure," he says easily.

We have hamburgers at least two or three times a month. I'm not a great cook, and I don't spend a lot of time on recipes. It's Idaho, and there aren't a whole lot of fast-food restaurants. So most of what we eat is what I make. Sometimes, Roy experiments in the kitchen, but cooking isn't something that he loves either.

I'm standing at the stove with a spatula in my hand, and he's slicing a tomato on a plate beside the onion he's already sliced.

Standing so close, it's made my eyes water, and I wipe at them before I say, "That was a pretty good game."

"That one ref was terrible," Roy says, using the back of his wrist to wipe his own eyes. Those onions are nasty.

"Yeah. I saw that. We won anyway. Which made me happy."

"Yeah. He was trying as hard as he could to help the other team. He might as well have picked up the ball and started shooting it."

"Surely someone would have said something about that," I say, turning the heat up a little bit on the hamburgers.

"I suppose. Did you see our point guard?"

I want to get on my knees right away and thank God I didn't have to figure out how to raise the subject. He did it for me. "She's good."

"Cute too."

"In a little, thirteen-year-old girl kind of way."

"Thirteen?" Roy turns his face to me. "Are you being serious?" He kinda hesitates, and there's clear disbelief in his voice.

"Mrs. Fry is her aunt. I made the comment that she was a good player, and in the course of our conversation, Mrs. Fry told me that she is only thirteen. She's the daughter of the coach."

"I knew that." Roy goes back to slicing a tomato, but I don't think he is really paying attention to what he's doing, because the slice he's working on is about an inch thick.

"I like tomatoes, but not that thick."

The knife stops. He says, "I didn't know she was that young."

"She's a good ballplayer," I say, trying to keep the conversation going, because I'm not sure exactly what he's thinking.

Is he shocked that she's thirteen and totally over her? Or is he shocked that she's thirteen and trying to figure out how they can still make it work?

I was a teenage boy once, too.

Right now, I kind of wish I hadn't been, because I know what I'd be thinking.

"She is good. I was the point guard for the team when I played three years ago. She handles the ball a lot better than I did."

"I imagine she's practiced a lot more than you have. If you're really interested in it, we can put a hoop up and a cement pad down here in the driveway. You can't get better if you don't practice." I mean that, and I'm not just saying it. If he's interested in basketball, I'm going to encourage that, even if I'm not interested.

"Really?" He looks over at me, like he can't even believe that I would say that.

Why not?

"Of course. I can't give you everything you want, and there are some things we just have to work for, like if we want to become a better ballplayer. But I'm your parent. If it's possible for me to provide a place for you to practice, you can bet I'm going to do it, if that's what you're interested in."

My son grins a little. "Thanks."

"I thought I might have seen you get Evie's phone number or some kind of contact info," I say as I flip a burger, striving for casual.

"I did. I didn't know how old she was, but I don't care," my son says, and his words are measured, like he knows they're not going to go over very well with me.

"She's not allowed to date."

"I didn't ask her out on a date."

I take a couple of breaths, not sure what else to say. And finally, I decide I'm just going to give it to him straight.

I turn the stove off and lean a hip against it, shoving a hand in my pocket and setting the spatula down on the stove.

My son looks at me, knowing it's kind of odd that I turned the hamburgers off in the middle of cooking them. He knows this is serious.

He gives me an uncertain look.

"You're not in trouble. I just want to say a couple things that maybe I should have said prior to this."

He lowers his brows, but at least he's looking at me with his head up and not peeking at me through the bangs that hang down over his forehead. "I just want to talk to her, Dad."

"I know. And I'm not telling you you can't. I'm just saying it can't be any more than that. Not right now. Because that's not what's best for Evie. She's only thirteen."

"I told you. I don't care how old she is."

"I understand you don't. But she has some growing up to do before she's ready to be thinking about having a boy in her life that is any more than a friend."

Roy's lips press together, but he doesn't argue with me. I'm pretty sure he agrees.

I'm not sure if he's ready for this now, but I figure it won't hurt. "I think sometimes we feel like we're in love. It's a feeling—a good feeling. But that feeling has to be backed up by actions, because eventually the feeling goes away. I know it's hard to imagine, and I understand. Just...if you truly care about her...if you truly care, then sometimes that means stepping back, even if it's not what's best for you or even what you want, but you do it because you know that's what's best for her."

Roy stares at my chest, and he breathes in and out more times than I can count.

I didn't tell him he wasn't allowed to do anything, and he's not in trouble, and I don't think he's angry at me. But he's processing what I said, I hope anyway, and I'm waiting to see if he's going to tell me that he agrees.

"I noticed her right away as soon as I started going to this school." Roy looks at me. "I've liked her for a really long time."

I nod. Those are facts I am not arguing with.

"The way I feel about her isn't going to change."

I nod again. This doesn't surprise me either. I suppose we all feel that way at some point in time. Maybe he's right; maybe he's not. The fact that he spent a year and a half watching her probably indicates he might be right.

"So I'm not sure if that's what you're saying or not, but I can't just decide I don't like her." He looks at me as though waiting for me to confirm that what he's saying is okay.

I have some opinions about that, but I don't think this is probably the time to get into them. "I'm not asking you to. I'm just asking you to wait. Because that's what's best for Evie. If you still feel the way that you do now when she's eighteen, then I'd say you probably have something."

"That's five years from now!" he bursts out.

"I'm not saying you can't talk to her or hang out with her. I don't know how old she has to be before she's allowed to date. But I kinda feel like if you like her as much as you seem to say you do, she's worth waiting for."

"What if she finds someone else in the meantime?"

"Then she wasn't meant for you," I say, and I know it's not the answer he wants to hear, but it's the answer I feel is true.

He has his lips pressed down. "So you're saying I'm allowed to message her, I'm just not allowed to date her."

"If her parents say you're not allowed to date her—if you want to do this right, you need to follow their rules—until she's eighteen at least. I would say if you want to have a good relationship with your in-laws, you'd better respect their rules even after that."

He nods, and the kid's not dumb. I know he understands most, if not all, of what I've said.

"I only wanted to talk to her anyway."

"That's fine," I say, and I think he's telling me the truth.

"And I guess I can ask her how old she has to be before she's allowed to date, although I don't even know if she's interested in me."

I could commiserate with that. I don't think this is the time though.

I have so many things I'd like to tell him, but I think that is enough for now.

I've done everything I can, for tonight, at least. Now I need to just hope that he respects me enough to listen to what I say, even if he doesn't completely understand.

I turn back toward the stove and turn the burner back on.

"Thanks for talking to me about it, Dad, and not yelling at me."

I look over at him, and I suppose he sees the confusion on my face. He shrugs.

"I guess Mom just always flipped out about everything."

"Because she loves you, son. That's the reason." That's not what I want to say, but I know it's the truth. She didn't treat me right, but I can hardly hold her mistakes against her, if I don't want the rest of the world to hold my many, many mistakes against me.

Forgiveness isn't easy, but I know it's the best way.

Badmouthing my ex to my son isn't the person I want to be.

"I guess you're right. I wish she had another strategy though," my son mumbles.

"Maybe she'll develop one," I say, and he smiles.

"Maybe you can be a good influence on her. Give her one of your stop-the-cooking-of-the-hamburger-so-you-can-turn-to-me-and-look-real-scary lectures."

I hit his arm with my elbow. "Are you messing with me, boy?"

"Maybe."

"Sure sounds like you're making fun of me."

"Take it how you want to," he says, grinning as he grabs the lettuce and starts to shred it.

Chapter 15

Tammy

I'm standing behind one of the tables that are set up in front of the fire station.

My mom's the fire chief in Good Grief, and while I'm not exactly the kind of girl that goes and fights fires or the kind of girl that goes and helps at a car accident, although that probably competes with rock slides for the thing they spend the most time doing, I do feel like it's important to support the local fire company.

They're all volunteers, and they all have full-time jobs.

Except Mom. She is a housewife and keeps Dad's books at the clinic and works there some, with the agreement that the fire company comes first.

My dad's pretty easygoing, and he's always supported Mom and whatever she's done.

I would have said this was a midlife crisis thing for her, because she started it when us girls were almost out of the house.

But honestly, she was born for the role and excels in it.

My sisters and I come and help wherever we can. Kori is the only one that's ever actually gone and fought a fire or responded to an accident. She has her first responders' certification and is actually pretty good at it.

I hate seeing people suffer, and I faint at the sight of blood, so it's definitely not the job for me.

Anyway, I'm the oldest and Claire is next to me, two years younger. She's here today, all smiles, because her fiancé is with her. Trey.

They're adorable together, and Trey looks at Claire like she's oxygen. I love it and I'm happy for her, even though sometimes when you're unhappy, it's hard to watch a couple be so happy together.

Leah and I are standing together behind the table selling daffodils. The funds go to benefit the ladies' auxiliary, which purchases everything from towels for the kitchen to equipment for the fire trucks.

We've even helped spring for a new—new to us anyway—fire truck.

Things are really busy when we first set up at nine o'clock. It is freezing cold too, so I appreciate staying active, but it's slowed down now that it's eleven, and Leah is telling me about the ladies in her assisted living center where she's the activities director.

Leah is a lot of fun and has great ideas, and she has an affinity for seniors, so she's perfect for her job.

I suppose people might say I'm boring and a stickler for details and have the strict demeanor that makes me perfect for my job too.

I don't think they mean it as a compliment.

"...and after the speaker gave her speech, the ladies went to bed, waited until the lights were out, then they got up, snuck outside, and gathered leaves off the trees in the yard, and they made what they called 'coverings,'" Leah uses air quotes for that word, "for themselves, and they all showed up for breakfast wearing them!"

She laughs, and I have to laugh along at the idea of those spunky eighty- and ninety-year-old women wearing "coverings" to breakfast at the assisted living center.

"So when I walked in, and I saw all these ladies in their 'coverings,' I knew there was only one thing I could do." Leah looks at me like I should know what the one thing was that she could do.

I have no idea. So I say, "And that was?"

"I went out and made myself a 'covering' too! And then I put it on! And we spent the day wearing our 'coverings.'"

"I hope that wasn't the day that the preacher came to speak in the auditorium," I say, and I don't smile even though I want to. Because the idea of the preacher seeing those coverings is just too rich.

I'm guessing they weren't made to specific modesty standards.

I suppose I could be wrong, but as I recall, the leaves on those trees at the nursing home are very small.

Leah's eyes twinkle. "No. But it was the day that we were scheduled to make a trip to Walmart."

"I bet that was interesting. Unlike with a preacher and his church, the ladies probably fit right in at Walmart."

"The supervisor wouldn't let the ladies out of the home unless they wore undergarments with their coverings." Leah said and she doesn't have to tell me, again, what she thinks of her boss. "Unfortunately, some of them were young ladies in the seventies, and they got kind of caught up in the whole covering thing, and they burned their undergarments."

"I'm surprised Mom wasn't called out to that one."

"Oh, she was," Leah said, her eyebrows raised.

Knowing our mom, I have to ask, "So, did she put the fire out? Or did she add her own undergarments to it?"

Leah chuckles. She knows Mom just as well as I do.

"She added to it, of course." Leah shakes her head. "I can't believe you didn't hear about it. What have you been doing? Living under a rock? Oh," she says without a pause. "I know. You have those term papers to grade."

"They're all graded. Except one," I say, and I don't add that that one's not even turned in yet.

"Another one of your pet projects?"

That's what Leah calls it when I spend extra time helping a student. She doesn't say it in an unkind way, but she does make a little bit of fun of my penchant toward not being able to stand to see anyone not pass my class. Short of doing the work for them, I'll do anything.

"I guess. He's a good kid that's just been through some hard times lately," I finally say, remembering that he also seems to have a crush on our niece, and I don't want to stigmatize him with Leah if he ends up becoming a part of our family. Hey, they're young, but you never know.

"He doesn't happen to be a kid who's been through some hard times and who happens to be living with a single dad?" Leah asks, not because she knows but because she always teases me about this.

She knows most of the time the kids that I help are living with single parents or grandparents, but it's never been anyone that I would be interested in.

Until now.

"Actually, yes," I say, and I watch Leah's eyes get big.

"Oh my goodness. It's happened. You've met a guy through your students. I always said that this would happen. When's the wedding?"

Now you have to understand Leah. She talks fast. Those are sentences she's saying, but they don't really sound like it. She's just one of those people that every single idea goes together, and you have to sort out in your head what she's saying while you're talking to her.

I grew up with her, so I'm kind of used to it. I can interpret pretty well, and most of the time, I get the main gist of what she's saying, if not all the details.

"I didn't say I was interested. I'm just saying that you're right. He's been through some hard times and is living with his dad. There's no mom."

I guess Leah's done teasing me, because her face falls. "That always makes me feel so bad."

I don't say anything, because my boys aren't living with their mom.

And it's hard on me. Probably not as hard on me as it is on them, but it feels like my heart has been shredded. It's been glued back together, I guess. But it's hard to go through something like that and not have a lot of scars to show for it.

Leah knows how I feel. Pretty much everyone knows how I feel. There were probably six months after my ex left and took my boys where I cried every single day. Most of the time, I didn't cry in the classroom. I did start wearing sunglasses while I taught.

I wasn't fooling anyone, but it made me feel better.

I'm better now.

I don't want to go through it again.

Suddenly, Leah is not looking at me anymore. Her eyes catch on something else. Someone else.

I figure it's a customer since she's looking toward the parking lot where the people park before they walk over.

"I've never seen him around here before," she says in a little voice. One that tells me she's talking about someone and she doesn't want them to hear.

I casually look over, expecting to see a tourist, although this isn't exactly tourist season. They do show up, occasionally. There is some beautiful country in Idaho.

But it's not a tourist. My heart wakes up and shakes itself off.

"That's him," I say, wishing I didn't have to but knowing he's probably going to at least see me and wave.

I'll have to explain everything to Leah anyway. I might as well fess up immediately. It'll make things less awkward in case he actually walks over to me to buy a flower. But there isn't anyone waiting at the other tables, and there's six or seven of us standing behind them, with me on the far end.

He'd have to walk past everyone else, and that would be pretty obvious.

I'm betting he won't. Why would he?

"That's him?" Leah says, emphasizing the "him."

"Yes. The guy I was telling you about, with the kid that I'm helping."

"Oh my goodness. You brushed me off, but I was right. That dude is..." Her voice trails off, and I can just hear the excitement deflating out of her. She ends, "...not the slightest bit perfect for you."

I'm not sure exactly what that means, but I don't take offense because it's my sister, and she doesn't mean to be hurtful, just honest.

Sometimes, it's annoying how honest siblings can be.

It's definitely annoying right now. I don't want her to be honest. I want her to say he's perfect for me, and he obviously likes me, and we are obviously meant to be together forever and always.

Wait. What?

I don't. I don't want that at all. That's ridiculous. I don't know why I was thinking that. I am not interested in Justin Gabriel.

And I don't want him to be interested in me.

All I'm interested in is helping his son pass my English class.

"Too bad, because he's the best prospect you've had in years." Leah's voice sounds fatalistic now, and she's messing with me.

I knock her shoulder with my hand. "Would you stop?" I notice that he walks by the first lady.

Of course Leah notices too.

"Oh my word. He's coming this way." She turns to me, her eyes wide. "I think he's coming to you."

She says this last really soft and right in my face before she turns around with a great big smile, even though she has no clue of his name, and just watches as he walks by her and stops in front of me.

Thankfully, he doesn't even look at her, so he doesn't see how dorky she looks with her great big smile and her look-at-my-big-sister hand gestures.

It's amazing that anyone ever wanted to date me, considering that I have three little sisters, and they all pretty much act like this, although Leah is definitely the worst.

She's far too old to act this way, too.

But I think there is something about being around your siblings that kind of brings out the child in you?

Maybe it's just my family.

"Good morning," Justin says. "I think the most beautiful flowers are down here on this end." He grins at me, casually, like he didn't just walk by six other ladies and stop in front of me.

And, just for the record, the daffodils in front of me are no different than the daffodils in front of everyone else. We unloaded them all off the same truck. Honest. I helped with that too, at an ungodly early hour this morning.

"Good morning, Mr. Gabriel," I say, aware of my sister staring at me.

Justin's eyes shift to my sister for just a fraction of a second before they come back to me. "So, we're back to Mr. Gabriel? I thought, after last night, we were on more familiar terms."

My eyes widen.

Leah has no idea he's talking about the basketball game.

She wasn't there. Sometimes, her job as activities director involves evening entertainment. I don't know for sure that's what happened, but I assume so.

Or maybe she was just busy buying undergarments for all the ladies who thought it would be fun to wear "coverings" all day.

I don't know.

"I had a good time last night," he says, and there is an undercurrent of something that is entirely inappropriate for the relationship that we have, which is barely friends.

Although he held my hand. And we did talk about a few personal things.

His tone is inappropriate—it's too intimate, and it makes my heart shiver. In a very good way.

That scares me.

Chapter 16
Justin

I don't know what it is about her that brings out the teasing in me. Or maybe it's just she brings out the truth.

I hadn't really intended to say the things I said, and I definitely hadn't intended to say them in the way I said them, and that's what I think made her eyes widen and her cheeks turn pink.

Which of course makes me want to tell her how cute she looks with pink cheeks, but a woman I assume is another sister judging by her looks and silent antics is standing beside her, and I've already embarrassed her enough.

Thankfully, four cars pull in almost at once, and suddenly the place that had been completely deserted is full of people, which I feel gives me a little bit more privacy, oddly, since her sister is now busy selling flowers.

"Did you get a chance to talk to Evie's mom?" I ask and hope that Tammy is still talking to me.

She nods, and her eyes flick to mine before moving away.

I've scared her. Not embarrassed her.

And immediately, I feel bad.

"I'm sorry," I say, meaning it sincerely and deeply. I want a lot of things from Tammy, but fear isn't one of them.

"What?" she asks, and I remember she's not used to anyone apologizing to her.

I want to call her ex a jerk, but we're all jerks at some point. Men especially.

We just need to find a woman who will forgive us.

Although, just because she forgives doesn't make it okay to keep being a jerk.

"I scared you. I didn't mean to. I guess I was trying to...flirt with you?" I grunt with self-consciousness. "I'm not very good at it."

She looks at me from under her lashes, and I remember what she said yesterday about tall girls, and I want to remind her how special it is that I'm taller than she is, but I also want to hear what she's going to say, so I don't say anything.

"So you're practicing your flirting on me?"

"No. The practice was already in my head. That was the real thing there."

I guess she gets what I'm saying, because it makes her smile.

I love her smile; it definitely feels good somewhere deep inside of me.

"I see." And I believe she does. I'm not practicing my flirting on her so I can use it on someone else. I practice alone because she's the one I want to use it on.

Funny, because I'm not really a flirting kind of guy. But for Tammy, I'll learn.

"So, can I ask what your sister said?"

"She's concerned, but she said that Evie's pretty serious about basketball, and she thought that's what they were talking about. She said Evie's not allowed to date until she's seventeen, but she's not gonna keep her from talking to boys."

I nod. "That sounds good. I actually went a little deeper with Roy, because I think he was a little bit more serious. Of course, he's older."

"Thank you. I think we've done what we could. I told Claire I would keep an eye on her but that I agreed with her. That there isn't anything to worry about, and that Roy is a good kid."

"He is. And I trust them. But I was also a young boy once, and I know there can be a struggle between knowing what he should do and doing what he wants."

"I think we all have that struggle," Tammy says, and one of her long fingers is tracing the narrow leaf of the daffodil.

"So, someone told me that I wasn't participating in community events and I should. So when I heard that there was something going on at the fire hall today, I had to come. I kinda thought it might involve food, and I'm a little disappointed that it's flowers. Inedible flowers."

"We can look it up. Maybe you can fry daffodil leaves or something. Dandelions are edible."

"I don't see any dandelions."

"People fry squash blossoms. I never had them, but..." She shrugs. "You put enough butter on something, and you can make pretty much anything edible."

"I'll take your word on that. I've never had squash blossoms, and I've gotta say I'm not exactly dying to try them."

"You're afraid to try new food?" she asks.

"Maybe I just need someone to hold my hand while I do it," I say, and she returns my smile, and I love that feeling, the feeling of sharing a joke with someone who gets you.

It's the feeling I've always had talking with her, after our initial meeting.

"I suppose you could look online for that. Maybe there are websites, people to hold your hand while you try new foods websites." She doesn't exactly bat her eyes, but she comes close.

"It's dangerous to find people on websites. It's much safer to find them at, oh, I don't know...the community fire hall. Or maybe church. Sometimes, you can pick up a good woman at a basketball game."

She's rolling her eyes now, but she's smiling, and I think she almost laughs which is definitely an improvement. There's still the cool reserve.

I think she might always have that. But I love the smile.

It kinda makes me feel good that she smiles for me.

"I'll keep all of that in mind. If I'm ever feeling the need to pick someone up who will hold my hand while I try new food. But I'm happy with the stuff I've tried, not really feeling the need to branch out."

"Really?" I say, and my tone makes her look at me.

She nods, figuring I've got something else to say.

"Funny, because I was feeling the exact opposite. But then, maybe I'm just looking for an excuse to hold hands with someone." I raise my brows. "Not just anyone." I do want to make sure she understands that.

I know other guys who pretty much try to see what they can get from every woman they meet.

That's never been me.

And, in my limited experience with women, it's not what they want.

I think Tammy and I feel the same way about that.

I know for a fact she's not that kind of girl. Not to be interested in a guy like that, and not to be a girl who does that kind of thing.

Not that I'm saying there's anything wrong with that. I just know it's not for me. And I'm happy that it's not for her either.

"Are we still on for tomorrow afternoon?" I ask.

"We sure are. I do hope that Roy is planning on working on his English before we work on the four-wheeler. I think that should be the order of things."

"I agree. And I can make sure, but I think he probably knows that."

She nods, and I say, "What time are church services tomorrow?"

"Which ones?" she asks with a sly grin.

"The ones the tall lady goes to. The lady who looks elegant, and who's a little scary, but I think she likes me." I say the last bit a little softly, like I'm sharing a secret with her.

"The tall lady? Is there only one in town?"

"I only have eyes for one," I say, and yeah, that's the kind of comment that might give me brownie points, but I wasn't even thinking that. I was just thinking the truth.

She doesn't call me on it. I think she knows I was being one hundred percent sincere.

"Sunday school starts at ten. Church eleven. The tall lady goes to both."

"Maybe the tall, *elegant* lady," I emphasize the word elegant, because I feel like that word suits her better than tall, "would be interested in being escorted to Sunday school?"

Her eyes go down, and she's touching the daffodil leaf again.

I feel like I need to reassure her. So I say, "As friends." I lean down a little and try to get her to look at me, tilting my head. "Maybe the man's asking because he wants a little more than that, but the man is willing to wait. For a long time." Just so she doesn't feel like she needs to rush into anything. The words are true as they're coming out of my mouth. I know it. I'll wait.

I had told Roy that love puts other peoples' needs and welfare above their own, and I believe that with my whole heart.

I don't want to wait. I want to move forward now.

But just like I told Roy, Tammy's worth it. To a teenager, five years feels like an eternity. To a man my age, five years feels like I don't want to waste another second of my life.

But there aren't a lot of women like Tammy around. And if I have to wait twenty years, I would rather do that than settle for something less.

I guess that's loyalty. Or maybe commitment. I'm not sure which, and it doesn't matter.

Maybe I should tell her, but I'm not sure I'm ready to say that yet. Even though I feel it.

"You might be waiting a very long time," she says softly. "And I don't want to do that to you. You deserve to have someone really special." She lifts her eyes, looks at me, and I know she means it. I kinda feel like this is her way of putting my needs first. I'm listening, and I'm liking what she says. "I don't want you to wait on something that might never happen. And I don't want you to feel like there's something wrong with you because I can't be more right away."

I shake my head. "I'll remember that, and I appreciate it. I do. I like what that says. But I also know what I want, and I know what I want is worth waiting for. Forever if necessary."

I don't want that. I don't want to wait forever. But I don't want a shadow of what I could have with Tammy, and that's what it would be if I were with anyone else.

She shakes her head. "Then you know where I live, and I leave for church at 9:45."

"I'll be there at 9:40. I'll have my son with me. Does that make it less appealing?"

I'm pretty sure I know her answer, but I needed to say that, because for the next three years at least, I come with a kid.

"It makes it more. I wish I could say the same thing." Her eyes drop again, and this time, I reach out and touch her chin just right at the base of it and press gently.

"Maybe someday you will." I say that, and I hope it with all my heart, but I also know it's not likely.

Her lips tilt up, but her eyes remain sad.

We stare at each other for just a few seconds, and I know I need to go. I've already spent too much time standing in front of her.

I drop my hand. "I'll take eight of these, but only if you help me carry them to my truck."

"Eight?" she asks, and I know she thinks she didn't hear me right.

"Yeah. I'm going to give them to my neighbor. She's eighty, and she thinks she's my mom. Which I don't mind, and last fall, I promised her I would clean out her flowerbeds, come spring. It's not quite spring, but if I am going to clean out her flowerbeds, I have the right to add a little bit to them."

"You can't go wrong with ladies and flowers," she says, tilting her head. "Especially flowers with roots and ones that will come back year after year."

I nod, having not really thought about it, but I suppose the flowers with roots represent something with permanence. Something you can look back on. Something that has memories for both of you.

"I think you're probably right," I say.

She tells me how much I owe her, and I take out my wallet and pay her in cash. I overpay by a couple dollars and tell her to keep the change, since it's for a good cause.

I don't do it to make a show, I just do it because it is right. And she is right, I should have been more involved in the community, instead of having my head stuck in my business all the time.

I need to make a couple of changes, regardless of whether I end up with Tammy or not.

She keeps her word and helps me carry the flowers to the pickup. We could have made it in one trip, but we take two.

I don't know about her, but I do it because it means more time with her.

I drive away, and I have to admit I'm a pretty happy man.

Chapter 17

Tammy

Justin is early on Sunday morning.

I'm happy to see that Roy is with him. I'm not sure how this is going to go down with Roy and Evie, but I like Roy, and I think, once he starts to feel comfortable in his new home in our community, he's going to be just fine.

It's probably a really awkward stage for a boy to have moved around so much. The early teen years are never easy, and he's had no stability.

Still, you don't get to choose the trials you're given.

You only get to choose what you make of them.

I hope he figures that out.

Nothing's worse than someone who thinks the world owes them because they didn't get a fair shake.

No one gets a fair shake.

I see that in kids all the time. It amazes me how some kids excel, despite their difficult circumstances.

If I hadn't been an English teacher, I might have studied psychology, just for that reason. It fascinates me that some kids have that ability.

I wish I did.

I wish I had the ability to put my rotten marriage behind me and embrace life with both arms, unafraid.

I wish, I wish, I wish.

But that's not me.

I'm hurt. And scared. And scarred. I just want to crawl into my shell and hide there.

The church building isn't far, and it's a warm day, so we walk. My mom lives in the house on the other side of the fire department building.

My sister Claire lives five houses down from her. I live on the other side of the street and the upper side of the fire department building.

It's nice to live so close to my family.

Most of the time.

Today though, I feel conspicuous, as my parents are walking to church, and so is Claire. Her girls are with her, and Trey is too.

He's asked her to marry him, but they haven't set a date. I expect the wedding to be soon. I like seeing them, I'm happy about it, but I'm definitely self-conscious with Justin beside me.

I don't want people to read more into this than I'm ready for them to.

"You could maybe act like you're not going to the guillotine," he suggests, with a little bit of humor in his voice, but I know he's serious.

"I'm sorry," I say, glancing up at him, and my features are not schooled, and my cool exterior has a crack in it.

Just walking with a man is outside of my comfort zone.

He walked me out of the basketball game, but it was dark.

This is a little different.

My sister and her family are walking maybe one hundred yards behind us, and Roy is behind us as well.

I suspect he's looking over his shoulder as often as he thinks he can get away with it. I sigh, a little sad, because he's so sweet, but Evie is too young.

Maybe they'll strike up a great friendship and be friends for years.

"That sigh sounded heavy," Justin says.

"I'm sorry. I was thinking about Evie and Roy." I glance over my shoulder to make sure he's not within hearing distance. He's fallen way behind. Halfway between us and them.

"They're way too young."

"I just hope everything works out for them."

I barely get those words out of my mouth when Mrs. Riley, the postmistress, steps out from the post office. She lives in the apartment above it, and as the postmistress, she knows everything that's going on in Good Grief and most of the surrounding communities.

I suspect, although of course I can't prove it, that she timed her arrival on the sidewalk to coincide with ours.

We are the hottest thing going on this Sunday morning.

"Oh my goodness. Tammy Harding. Who *are* you walking with?" Mrs. Riley falls into step beside Justin—again I believe it's by design.

Who wouldn't want to walk beside him?

I don't correct her incorrect use of my name. I'd rather be Harding than Fry anyway, and I've meant to change it for years, but...I haven't.

"Mrs. Riley, this is Justin Gabriel. He owns the four-wheeler shop between here and Ravens Point."

"Oh. No wonder we haven't met."

"And, Justin, this is Mrs. Riley. She's the postmistress in Good Grief."

"Nice to meet you, ma'am," Justin says, very politely and respectfully. It makes me feel a little bit more comfortable and even more proud to walk beside him. "It's a lovely town. Have you lived here long?"

"All my life. And it *is* a lovely town." Mrs. Riley has a tendency to emphasize her verbs. "Why, Good Grief is probably one of the best towns in Idaho, if not the top of the list. We definitely have the best volunteer fire company."

Mrs. Riley looks around the front of Justin, at me. "I'm sure you already know that Tammy's mother is the fire chief. And, I might add, Tammy is one of our best citizens. You'd better snatch her up fast, because she's very eligible and *very* in demand."

That time, she emphasizes an adverb. I wonder at the change.

My brows shift down, and my eyes narrow. I try to look at Mrs. Riley across the front of Justin, but she's not meeting my gaze.

Half of me wants to laugh, and half of me wants to stamp my foot.

I know what Mrs. Riley is doing. At least I think I do.

She knows I've been single for a long time, and she's trying to help me get out of that sorry state.

Never mind I might not want to.

Although maybe I do.

"Tammy is an excellent teacher at our high school, and she comes from a very reputable family. Her father is a veterinarian," Mrs. Riley says, lowering her voice a little bit like she's letting him in on the family secrets.

Justin is nodding his head, a little smile around his mouth, and I think he has Mrs. Riley figured out too.

I sigh. Am I going to stand here and take this, or am I going to say something?

I lean in front of Justin. "Mrs. Riley?"

"Yes, my dear?" Mrs. Riley says, very benevolently.

I sigh. She's enjoying herself, and she's not hurting anything, even if she is making me feel like a horse on the auction block.

I say, "Never mind."

Justin leans down—he doesn't have far to lean—and he whispers in my ear, "Chicken."

I shake my head, and I lift my mouth up. He barely has to move, and I'm whispering in his ear. "No. You just can't fight the tide."

"Remember that," he whispers back.

And I feel like he's saying something different. Maybe like he *is* the tide.

I think about the ocean. I've been there once. It moves me, probably like it moves everyone that looks at it. And I think again about the kids in my classroom, some who come from really terrible circumstances but thrive anyway.

They aren't afraid of life and meet it with arms wide open, facing the challenges and conquering them.

Why can't that be me?

Chapter 18

Tammy

I don't die in church.

Not from embarrassment and not from excitement at actually having a really fantastic man sitting beside me.

And yes, I can admit that Justin is really fantastic.

He sits with the proper distance between us, but he also puts his hand on the back of the pew.

It's not exactly around me, since his hand is kind of in the middle of my back, but I love it nonetheless.

Maybe this means my life up until now is really pathetic, that I hadn't realized how wonderful it would feel to be sitting beside someone that I really, really like, and he looks at me like he likes me too.

I hate to compare him to my ex, but my ex never went to church with me, and when we did go places together, he never seemed to be very interested in me.

He didn't look at me like I was fascinating, and he didn't treat me like he cared what I wanted or even what I was doing.

Yes. I wonder sometimes too why I married him.

I don't know. He was taller than I was. What can I say?

I think that one church service where all Justin does are the things I just mentioned—put his arm around me, act like he is interested in me, look at me like he likes me, and I guess I didn't mention it, but a couple of times, he leans over and whispers in my ear, just a comment on something the preacher said, and I whisper back and we have our own little private conversation, one that feels intimate and warm—is all he needed to do.

That one church service does more to make me fall in love with him than anything else he's done.

Maybe I haven't fallen completely in love, but I am on my way. That service is a huge push.

I admit, on the walk back to my house, I'm kind of dreamy. You know, when you're really happy and just can't imagine life getting any better?

I don't walk around in a state like that very much.

Ever. I don't walk around in a state like that ever.

Oh boy, am I ever walking around in a state like that on my way home from church.

We are chatting about nothing, different types of trees, I think, not that it mattered. We're just happy to talk to each other, and we care about each other's opinions. Maybe that sounds boring, but with the right person, it is definitely fun.

And then Justin's phone rings.

I admit I don't pay too much attention to his conversation at first. It really isn't any of my business, and as much fun as I am having with him, I have to remind myself that he isn't mine, and I don't have any right to butt into his business.

I mean, I kind of hope what we are doing is going somewhere.

I want it to go somewhere, but we haven't talked about it, and again, his phone call isn't any of my business.

But my head comes down out of the clouds as I realize he's frustrated.

"Are you sure?... Yes, I know... Right... No, I can handle it... Yeah, I'll be there in twenty... Yeah, I can do that... See you then."

I think it is the "I'll be there in 20" that really gets me.

Obviously, he is leaving.

I guess a part of me wants to say, I knew it was too good to be true. I knew it wasn't going to last. But another part of me says, why am I getting so upset? We can have more times like this.

"Braden didn't show up for work this morning at noon when the shop opened. That is the other salesperson—the one you met. There are three customers there, and he's panicking." Justin shoves a hand in his pocket, and his whole body posture says that he is frustrated and doesn't want to say this, but he says, "I need to go."

"That's fine." I don't mean it is "fine" as in I don't care. I mean it is fine as in I understand that he has to go. It is his business, and it pays his bills, I assume, so I can hardly be upset, can I?

"I want to ask you to come with me, but..."

I look over my shoulder, and Roy is coming along behind us.

My sister and her girls are nowhere to be seen. I feel a little bad for Roy, but he's young, he's got time.

I suppose I have time now, too. "I promised Roy that I would help him with his English and that I would let him help me with the four-wheeler. I really can't go today."

"I know. That's what I was gonna say. I know Roy's been looking forward to helping you. I think he thinks it's going to be fun to help his English teacher learn how to ride an ATV."

"I'm glad he thinks so," I say, and while I'm truly not looking forward to it, I'm not dreading it either.

I did buy it, so I might as well learn how to ride it.

"I'm just disappointed, because I thought it'd be fun too," Justin says, and his voice drops on that last bit, using that tone that makes a shiver sparkle at my backbone.

I like that too.

I look over at him, still feeling warm from having him beside me in church, and he's looking down at me, and I believe every last word—he really doesn't want to leave me.

It blows my mind.

I can't believe that someone like him, someone successful, funny, kind, and thoughtful, would be the slightest bit interested me.

I admit I have a hard time figuring it out.

I know what that says about me, but after being shredded by my ex, I guess I can't blame myself.

"I'm disappointed too. A lot," I say, knowing I'm an English teacher and I should have better words than that to explain to him how crushed I am to think of spending the afternoon without him when I had been looking forward to being with him all day so much.

He doesn't seem to mind that my words aren't eloquent. They make him smile. Not in a happy way but in the "I'm glad you said that because it made me feel good" kind of way.

It's funny, but I like making him feel good.

We're at my house, and he didn't leave anything inside, so he walks me to the door, and with his hand on the knob, he says, "I guess I'll leave Roy here."

He looks over his shoulder at Roy who's just walking down the sidewalk in front of my house.

"That's fine. I'll make sure he gets home."

"I appreciate it. He'll know I get off work at six, but you can remind him of that if he asks."

"I will."

"Thanks for not being mad at me."

This puzzles me. "Why would I be mad?"

He lifts a shoulder and shifts his feet. "I don't know. It always made my ex angry when things would come up with the business, things I didn't have any control over and had to take care of. I guess she got tired of it, but it made her mad from the beginning."

"I see. If this happened every Sunday, I would. Especially if you promise to spend every Sunday with me, knowing that you're probably getting called to work..."

"Really, this doesn't happen every Sunday. In fact, this is the first time that employee hasn't shown up. I'm betting he has a good excuse."

"Probably. I hope it's nothing serious."

"If I find out, I'll let you know."

"Thanks."

He gives me another look, then he opens the front door for me. "Thanks for letting me go to church with you. I enjoyed it."

I don't know what my face looks like when I turn around and say, "Me too." But I know those words don't convey nearly what I feel.

I don't think I can say anything more, though. We're not really at that point in our relationship. If we ever get there.

Like I said, it's hard for me to believe that he is that serious about me.

Part of me wants to do a background check and see if he is on some kind of parole or something.

Part of me thinks that's mean and completely unnecessary, and I should have better self-confidence than that.

That does happen to women.

He shakes his head and kind of grunts. "I don't even want to know what you're thinking. It looks like it could start a whole other conversation."

I laugh. "It's nothing important, I promise you."

"Have a good afternoon."

"You too," I say, and he kind of rolls his eyes because, hello, he's going to work.

I shut the door behind me, seeing that Roy has met him at the back of his truck, and they chat for little bit. I have gone to the kitchen and started getting lunch before Roy knocks on my door.

I thought he would just walk in; I go and open it.

"Come on in, Roy. I'm going to change, and we'll eat a little lunch. Then we'll get your English out. Does that sound good?"

"How long do we have to work on English before I start teaching you how to drive the four-wheeler?" Roy asks eagerly.

"How about we work the same amount of time on your English as we work on the four- wheeler?"

He nods. That's fair.

"An hour?" he asks.

"That's fine with me."

He hasn't brought any other clothes to change into, but he's wearing a T-shirt and jeans along with boots, so he doesn't need them.

I come back downstairs, and we have simple meatloaf sandwiches from leftover meatloaf that I'd had during the week.

He doesn't complain and eats it like he hasn't eaten in a week, which is how I think fifteen-year-old boys typically eat, not that I've seen my boys eat much.

The thought makes me sad, so I push it away. I don't want to be melancholy the whole time I'm with him.

I wasn't sure whether an hour would be enough, but we get a lot done on his English. I'm able to help him see how he can organize his information, and one of the best things about teaching is, as I'm explaining, I see the light dawning in his eyes. It's so encouraging to see what I'm saying is resonating with him and he's getting it.

So yes, it is a very rewarding hour for me.

But then it's time for us to go out and do the four-wheeler thing.

I know this is not going to be nearly as rewarding, but I also know I need to have a good attitude.

Chapter 19

Tammy

I grab the keys off the hook, and I lead the way outside.

I live in town, and I am a little concerned my neighbors are going to have a comedy show to watch in my yard this afternoon.

I try to put that thought out of my head. Both of my neighbors are nice people, and if I can provide some entertainment for them and a few laughs, I guess I shouldn't hold it against anyone.

We get out to the four-wheeler, and I stop beside it. Just stand there staring at it.

I think I can get on it, but that is the only thing I know how to do. And I've never done that, despite my intentions to at least practice sitting on it.

"So... I usually get on it before I start it," Roy says, and I know he's feeling like he's a little out of his element.

Part of that is probably because I'm his English teacher, and he's not used to telling me what to do. Part of it also, and I'm just guessing here, is that he's never met anyone quite as ATV stupid as I am.

I put my left foot on the bottom step, or whatever it is, and I immediately realize that I should put my right foot down, because my left foot needs to go over.

So, I step up, put my right foot down, and swing my left leg over.

First move, and I already look like a ninety-year-old.

But I didn't get hurt, I didn't run over anything, and I didn't wreck the thing, so... I'm counting it a win.

I think Roy is biting back a smile. I want to help him.

"Roy?"

"Yeah, Mrs. Fry?"

"If I do something stupid, you're allowed to laugh at me." I turn and look at him. "Okay?"

"You're not going to flunk me if I laugh at you?"

"I am looking for every excuse in the world to not flunk you. You are allowed to laugh as much as you want. I promise." At this, the grin he's been biting back lifts up his face.

I knew it.

By the time we are done, I'm sure I'll be laughing at myself, so he might as well get a jumpstart on me.

His finger comes out, and he points at a hole in what would be the dashboard if it were a car. "This is where you put the key."

"Got it." I say, putting the key in and able to do that without too much trouble. I do that in my car all the time. At least I used to, but the car I bought two years ago is keyless.

"So...you want to flick the switch to 'run,' and you want to make sure your gearshift is in neutral." He touches the switch as he talks about it which I flick to "run." It's written right underneath the switch.

And then he shows me the gearshift, and he actually points to the "N," which I assume stands for neutral.

Again, I've got the shifter in my car, which is very similar, so up to this point, I'm feeling pretty good.

"Then you turn the key."

"Okay. I think I got it." I turn the key, and the motor chugs, then fires up.

I want to do a fist pump, but I *am* his English teacher, so I don't.

But the thought is there.

I think he wants to climb on with me, but again, it's that whole English teacher thing, so he just shows me how to put it in drive, shows me where the brake is, which he seems to think is pretty important, as do I, and then he says, "All you do is give it a little gas." And he shows me where the throttle is.

Wow. I actually think I can do this.

I'm not the best in the world at driving a car, but I've never had an accident, and actually, I'm a pretty safe driver. Maybe I'm good.

I even drive in the snow.

When you live in Idaho, you pretty much have to be able to drive in the snow.

That's why I have an SUV.

The smallest SUV they make, but an SUV nonetheless. You really can't live in Idaho and travel to work and not have one.

So I start out going really slow, but by the time we've spent an hour at it, I'm feeling pretty confident. Roy never does climb on behind me, but he walks alongside me, which I admit makes me nervous and comforts me at the same time.

I take a look at my phone and then park the four-wheeler where we started.

"Our hour is up, and it flew by." Nobody is more surprised than I am.

"That was kind of fun, Mrs. Fry. You did a good job."

Okay, maybe Roy is surprised that I did so well. He definitely sounds like it.

I turned it off and swing a leg over. "That wasn't as bad as I thought it was going to be. You're a good teacher, Roy."

He beams under my praise which makes me smile. I really like his dad, and I like him too. He's a good kid.

"So are we gonna do this tomorrow after school?" Roy asks.

I think for a minute. If we do it after school, Justin probably won't be with us.

But maybe that is for the best. I don't think Justin would step on his son's toes or push in and try to teach me himself. And I know he wouldn't get in the way when I'm trying to teach Roy about his term paper, but I think that as much as I would like to have Justin with me, maybe this should be something that just Roy and I do.

I really shouldn't use it as a way to see Justin.

"We could do that. You can come to my classroom directly after your last class, we can work on your term paper, and then we'll drive here. I'll feed you." I might not have my boys with me, but I do know boys need to eat. It makes Roy smile.

I make a mental note to go to the grocery store before school to make sure I have something to feed him. "And then we'll work on the four-wheeler for an hour."

"That sounds good, except..." His voice trails off, and I study him, trying to figure out what he's trying to say. Finally, he mumbles at the ground, "Maybe we ought to move your four-wheeler to our property, because there's a lot more room there."

I could be wrong, but I think that he's afraid to make a suggestion I might not like.

"That's a great suggestion. I love it. Maybe your dad would do that?"

He nods. "If you give me the key for your four-wheeler, and I promise I won't lose it, I'll give it to Dad and maybe he can do it on his way to work tomorrow morning."

Disappointment deflates my chest. I was kind of hoping that he might come and do it tonight, and I would get to see him. I hold the key out to Roy. "Sounds good to me. Do you think he'll mind?" I ask as an afterthought.

"I know he won't. He wants you to learn too. You need to be able to drive at least a little bit better in order to go on the charity run."

This scares me, because I thought Justin wouldn't have suggested it if he thought it was too far above my skill level.

Maybe he was counting on me getting better. Or maybe he didn't know how bad I was when he suggested it.

I say, "I appreciate it. Thank you."

"No. Thank you," Roy says, and we share a look. Not exactly a "we're friends" look, but definitely a "we're comfortable with each other" look, and he takes my key, and we go to my SUV, and I take him home.

Chapter 20

Justin

Normally when I get called into work, I don't mind at all.

When you're self-employed, your work is your business, and you own it. Everything I do at my job helps make my business better.

I want to be successful, and I don't mind putting the time and the work into making it that way.

At least, I never have.

But I've never had the opportunity to spend time with someone like Tammy either.

I was actually angry when I got called into work. Which is a first for me.

I did not want to go.

I was so close to telling the kid to just close the shop and go home.

Even with three customers waiting.

But that's not the way I do business. It never has been. I want my business to be successful, don't get me wrong about that, and I'm always looking at the bottom line, and the goal is to make money. But I also have a goal of being the kind of business that people talk about in a good way. Because of the great service they get, because of the great prices I give them, and because I'm honest and forthright. Basically, I want to run the kind of business that I want to go to.

I want to treat people the way I want to be treated.

That's the bottom line.

Now obviously, I can't stay in business if I don't make money, so there is that, but it's more than just money. It always has been.

If I'm not doing some good in the world, if I'm not doing good for the people that I'm serving, then I might as well not have a business.

But a man has to do something to make a living.

Still, it was hard as anything to walk away from Tammy.

I need to put some kind of system in place so that if there is a problem, I'm not the only one that can fix it.

I'd never seen the need for that before, because I'm always available. I don't even take vacations. What is the point in going on vacation by myself?

Maybe in a few years, Roy will be interested in getting into the business more than he already is. He does a good job when he is here, but his school needs to come first.

I think of Evie. He has a social life too.

I am bummed when he's home when I get off work.

I might have been tempted to take my truck and run over and get Tammy's four-wheeler immediately, hoping to see her, but he tells me that she is visiting her nieces tonight. That's what she told him when she dropped him off.

Of course, Roy is saying this because he's thinking of Evie, but I'm thinking there's no point going over and getting her four-wheeler because I'm not going to see her.

I might see her in the morning.

Turns out I don't.

She's already left for school when I pull in. At least, her SUV isn't there.

I should have gone earlier. I know she's conscientious and can't stand to be late. But I had no idea that she'd leave for school before seven in the morning.

The kid who works for me really did have a legitimate reason to not show up for work. His appendix burst.

He ends up being off the rest of the week.

Which meant I work late every day.

Thursday is the only day we are open super late, but spring is a busy time of year for ATV sales, and I don't have any time to catch up on paperwork during the day. So after I shut down at night, I have to do the paperwork.

That means I don't see Tammy all week.

I do dig for some information from my son. Which probably isn't the most ethical thing to do, but I am a desperate man.

He tells me she is doing well with her ATV skills and that she is running the trail behind our house.

As long as she can run that, she can do whatever the charity run has. She isn't going to place or anything, but I don't think she cares about that.

I wish I was there to watch her though.

Honestly, I am just happy watching her. I enjoy talking to her, too.

I should have gotten her phone number. I wish I had.

By Wednesday night, I've managed to hire a temporary employee to fill in for me. I spend some time on Thursday training him, so Friday night, I'm able to leave.

Roy has texted me and told me that he's shooting at the gym, and he had a ride there. But he needs a ride home. And I am to pick him up at eight.

That means I'm going to eat supper by myself.

Instead of stopping at my house after I'm done with work, I drive into Good Grief, heading for the Lone Pine Tavern.

I drive by Tammy's house first, but her car isn't there.

I know she said she spends a lot of time with her nieces, and I think that maybe she might be with them, but while I'm brave enough to stop unannounced at her house, I'm not brave enough to just show up at her nieces' house and...do what?

How would I explain my presence there?

So I pull into the Lone Pine Tavern. I've already placed an order for fries, planning on taking them home and eating them there, so I walk in to pick them up.

There's one person in line in front of me, and I recognize the basketball coach that was coaching with Tammy's sister.

Trey.

Apparently, he was a big thing when he was in high school, an all-state baller or something.

I didn't grow up around here, so it doesn't mean as much to me.

I didn't play basketball, so even though someone said he was all-state, I have no idea what that means.

Still, he turns around and looks as he hears a door jingle, and he gives me a friendly grin, which I return.

"Hey, man," he says, holding his hand out.

I did see him in church, but we didn't talk.

Still, I respond. "Hey. What's up?" I shake his hand.

He has a firm grip and looks me in the eye. I like that. "Not much. I'm baching it tonight, because your woman's with mine."

This makes my brows go up.

Obviously, he notices, but he doesn't comment on it.

My woman?

I've not thought of Tammy that way.

I'm not even sure if we are really friends. I haven't talked to her all week.

But he is calling her "my woman."

Sounds kinda cavemanish, but I gotta admit there's a part of me that likes the caveman thing.

As much as I want to pretend I know what he's talking about, I can't. So I say, "Oh really?"

He nods. "They're having a girls' night. Didn't she tell you?"

One side of his face creases up, and I know he's laughing at me. Or maybe he's laughing at Tammy for not having enough nerve to tell me that she's having a girls' night. I don't know.

"No. She didn't."

"Doesn't surprise me too much. Tammy plays close to the vest. Her ex did a real number on her from what Claire says. Still, she talks about you all the time. She's really got it bad."

So now I want to blink owlishly at him, but I don't. I just want him to keep talking. "She does?" I ask, hoping this prompts him to say more.

"She can't say enough good about you." He lifts his shoulder and grins a little. "I actually did a background check on you. Checked out your business. Hope you don't mind. I'd expect you to do the same thing for Tammy's sisters. Their dad's a nice man, but he's pretty easygoing, and I didn't know whether you were a serial killer or not."

Part of me wants to be offended, but part of me appreciates this. So I say, "Thank you. I'm glad to know that someone's got her back. She's alone."

I don't say anything about her boys and how that hurt her, but Trey seems to already know, and he nods.

"She deserves a good man," he says. He doesn't exactly say that I am a good man, but I think it's implied.

"I agree. Someone better than me." And I mean that. That's not a false modest putdown. She does deserve someone who's not going to leave her on Sunday afternoon because they have to run into work.

"Nobody's perfect." Trey gives me another look. "But you checked out okay, and she really likes you. I hope you don't hurt her. I've never seen her with someone other than her ex, and this is a pretty big deal for her."

"It's a big deal for me, too." And I'm not kidding about that. I know we're different. I like to be outside, although I haven't been lately with getting things set up for work, but I'm really looking forward to the charity run next week. Not just because I get to be out, but because I'll finally get to see Tammy again.

"Glad to hear it. She's not the kind of woman that plays games."

I nod. I already know this.

Trey's order's up. He turns back around and steps forward to the counter.

I think about what he said, and I have to say, it's encouraging. I think Tammy might like me. I hadn't been sure about that, but after listening to what Trey had to say, I'm thinking she really does. And not just a little. Like I might be someone she's serious about.

I do something then that I've never done before. And I don't recommend it.

I drive by the school, and I see my son playing basketball with a group of kids.

It doesn't surprise me to see Evie among them. I laugh, because she must not have wanted to be involved in the girls' night.

I guess I know what it's like to be consumed with something, and Evie seems to be consumed with basketball.

Roy seems pretty interested in it too, but I know Roy is more interested in Evie than he is in basketball. Funny how a girl will do that to a guy.

Thankfully, when Roy sees me pull in, I don't have to walk over, because he jogs over to my pickup.

I get out and stand beside my door. "Do you have Mrs. Fry's phone number?"

I realize now I could have just texted him for it. It shows how messed up I am that I stopped at the school in order to get it.

I've definitely got this bad. I'm laughing at Roy for playing basketball for Evie, and here I am checking my brain at the door, driving around without it.

Roy gives me a look, but he says sure, and he jogs back over to his stuff, grabs his phone, and hurries over to me.

He pulls it up, clicks on it, and texts it to me. "Is that all you wanted?"

"Yeah. Thanks."

"Is there a problem?" Roy asks, and he looks worried.

"No. Did your driving lesson go okay today?" It still irks me a little that they've been doing them after school and I haven't seen Tammy drive at all.

"It did. And I just have a little bit more work to do on my term paper. I might have it finished Sunday afternoon if I work hard. Mrs. Fry seems pretty happy with it."

"I'm glad."

"Well..." He scuffs his foot on the blacktop. "If you don't need anything else, I'm going to run back over. They're waiting on me."

Indeed, the game has stopped, and kids are chugging from their water bottles and standing around.

I notice that Evie doesn't laugh and joke with the boys, and I like that. I really didn't have any doubt that she is here to play basketball and not flirt, but I know there are some girls who would play basketball just to be around boys.

I suppose there's nothing wrong with that, but I'm glad Evie isn't that kind of girl.

"I'll pick you up at eight," I say, and Roy gives me a wave before he runs back over.

I'm not even sure what I'm going to say to her. As desperate as I am to actually stop at the school and get her number, I don't even know if I can text her. I need some kind of excuse, since I can't just text her out of the blue.

Or can I?

Chapter 21

Tammy

I had to get your number from Roy. It's Justin.

The text startles me. No one ever texts me. My sisters are deep in a discussion about Leah's boss. He's giving Leah a hard time at her job, and they don't notice my secret smile as I realize the text is from Justin.

If I can't stop smiling, my sisters are going to notice.

I hold my phone in my lap while my thumbs fly over the screen.

I would have given it to you if you would have asked.

There is a lot of flirt in that. Hopefully, it doesn't make it through the airwaves. Melody is with us, as well as her mother, Claire, and my other sister Leah.

We painted our toenails and gave ourselves facials, and now we're just hanging out drinking soda and eating junk food.

They're eating. I'm really not.

Although, I have to admit I've been eating a little more lately, and I'm not sure if it's because of being outside with Roy, practicing on the four-wheeler, or just because of knowing that Justin likes me a little.

Likes me. For me.

I'm not even sure how to explain it, but it does something to my confidence when I know that someone looks at me and sees someone they want to hang out with and do things with.

Someone they like so much they get my phone number from their kid.

"Why are you smiling?" Kori asks.

Of course, they see me. I don't usually go around with a goofy grin on my face.

Kori is sweet and spunky, and typically she flits from job to job to job.

She was a firefighter for a while with Mom, but that doesn't pay anything. She just did it for the thrill.

She truly cares about people, don't get me wrong, but she gets bored easily.

She probably has ADD, not that it was ever diagnosed.

"Was I smiling?" I ask, not in my heartiest tone, but in my "I'm older than you and I can still beat you up" tone.

I guess sometimes the things you do as kids you never quite outgrow.

Not that I ever beat any of my sisters up, but being the oldest does have perks.

Being the biggest pretty much all of your childhood does too.

With my height, I was always the biggest.

"You were, and now you're trying to pretend you weren't." Kori narrows her eyes. She's not going to let me get away with it. I suppose that's from being the youngest sister. She was babied, and she's fearless. "So spill."

I shrug. "Justin just texted me."

I feel stupid, because he didn't even say anything funny. I am just smiling because it was him.

My phone buzzes, and all of my sisters lean toward me. Even Melody gets caught up in it.

I give them all the haughtiest look I can muster before I look at my phone.

I couldn't ask because I haven't seen you all week.

I don't tell my sisters what he said, and I keep my phone close to my chest as I text back.

I've been at your house every day. Where have you been?
I'm here now. Waiting on you.

"So how serious are you and Justin?" Claire asks, with her brows raised.

I've talked to my sisters about him. They know I like him. Seems like every time we get together, that's all I want to talk about.

It's all I want to think about.

Sometimes, I even catch myself thinking about him while I'm teaching English.

I suppose everyone needs to dream.

I haven't allowed myself to dream for so long, though, I feel almost consumed with this one.

I definitely do not like that. I don't want to be consumed with anything. It's too hard to rebuild out of the ashes.

"They must be pretty serious if she's texting him," Leah says. They know I don't usually do this. Don't *ever* do this.

Melody's here, my niece, but she's really not interested in manicures or pedicures or facials or anything like that. Even though we try to get her to do this with us, she gets bored easily, like now—with the adults all focused on my phone, she's taken the opportunity to wander out into the kitchen with a chemistry book open, and if I know Melody, she's probably getting into an experiment.

Since we're at Kori's house, I'm not too concerned about it.

Not that I wouldn't let her at my house. I just know there might be a smell associated with it—speaking from experience—which might give me a pang or two.

But my niece is worth it.

"Trey looked him up," Claire says, her face serious. "For some reason, Trey was concerned that he was like, I don't know, a serial killer or something. Men think differently than we do, I guess."

The thought had run through my head. I might have been concerned he was a pedophile, but I don't have my boys, so he wouldn't be picking on me. He'd find some single woman with children.

No, Justin being a pedophile isn't the thing I have to worry about.

"What did he find?" I ask, but I'm not worried. Maybe he's a serial killer. Everyone always says, "he just didn't seem like the type. He was such quiet neighbor." All that, but I've seen his business, and I've seen his son. I've been to his house, and I've seen the flowers that he planted in the neighbor's flowerboxes. I know he is exactly what he says he is.

Still, I wait for Claire's answer.

"Clean as a whistle. He does have several businesses other than the four-wheeler place that's outside of town. I know exactly how much he paid for it if you want to know. And I can give you the name and address of his ex. I can also give you the name of her current husband and their two small children."

"Wow. That was pretty thorough."

"You can find out a lot on social media nowadays."

"Is Justin on social media?" I hadn't even considered. I quit social media when I got divorced. I suppose that would be a better way to keep up with my kids, but I Snapchat them every night, and we FaceTime each weekend.

That's all I get, and it's not nearly enough.

"No. But his ex is. And her husband. That gave us enough juice to get started." Claire shrugs. "Plus, Trey's good at that stuff."

"I appreciate it," I say, and I suppose that's true. "I'm not sure that exactly tells us he's not a serial killer though. If we knew that, he'd be in jail, right?"

"Good point, Tammy," Kori says, popping up from her chair and padding out to the kitchen, opening the refrigerator door. "Does anyone want anything?"

We all chorus "no thank you," and she brings herself in a soda before tucking her leg underneath her and plopping down on the chair.

Every movement she makes is quick and jerky, like she's a live wire that just can't quite contain itself.

"We are talking about Leah and the issues she's having with her boss. I don't think we solved that problem yet," I say, a little sarcastically, because we always joke that we talk about things but never solve anything. Still, it makes us feel better.

"There's nothing to solve. He needs to go," Leah says, and I know she means it. "I think I figured out how to make that happen."

Claire raises a brow. "And are you going to tell us?"

"No. Because if I get arrested, I don't want you guys to go down with me."

I think she's kidding. But she seems to have gotten to the end of a rope with her boss, so maybe she's not.

At least they get back to talking about Leah, and I glance at my phone. It had buzzed when Claire started talking about looking Justin up on social media, but I hadn't gotten a chance to look at it. Maybe because things are still new, or maybe because that's just the way I am, but probably because of the debacle of my last relationship, I just want to keep this low-key for now.

I'm with my sisters.

I know. I talked to Trey.

Oh? He was in the store?

I saw him at the Lone Pine Tavern when I was picking up my fries.

He looked you up.

I say this because I don't want Justin thinking it was my idea. I definitely don't want him to find out and think I approved it. Although, I guess if they'd asked me if I wanted them to, I might have said yes. A girl can't be too careful.

He told me he did. I'm glad. I hope it eases your mind.

It wasn't my idea. But I did find out about it tonight.

He told me...you talk about me all the time. Is that true?

Oh wow. I finger my phone. My sisters' chatter goes on over my head. It feels dangerous to admit this. Especially after not talking to him all week. I guess there's a part of me that thinks if he really wanted to see me, he would have made sure he did.

Even though I know when a person has a business, they have to take care of it. I wouldn't want him to be less than that.

Still, I don't exactly feel neglected or anything, but I wonder about his sincerity.

Of course, he could probably wonder the same thing about me, because I haven't gone out of my way to see him.

I could have lingered at his house. After all, I was there every day. And I hadn't.

Maybe I'm just one of those women that want to be chased.

That seems kind of immature.

Still, I guess the idea is if someone likes me enough to chase me, I know they really like me.

But this isn't about me. He is asking if it is true, and I'm not going to lie.

My thumbs move much more slowly as I type out this text.

Maybe. I guess everyone says I do. You are kind of interesting.

Just a couple minutes after I send this, Leah stands up. Justin hasn't replied, and I'm afraid I've scared him off.

"I have to work tomorrow. It's box-store run day. Hopefully, we don't have the debacle with the coverings that we did several weeks ago. That's what really did it in with my boss." She rolls her eyes, and I catch something in her expression that makes me look twice.

Maybe if I hadn't been involved the way I am with Justin, I would have missed it. But...I think she might have a thing for her boss.

I stand up with her, fingering my phone which just buzzed. I'm ready to go. I love spending time with my sisters, but I'm feeling restless, and I just want to walk.

We say goodbye, and Leah and I head out together, chatting about Mom. She didn't make it tonight because there was an accident on the interstate at our exit.

We aren't the main company involved, but she is doing traffic control.

We separate at our vehicles. Then I get in and start mine before I look at my phone.

I find you interesting too.

That text makes me smile, and then another one comes in. Like he had to think about it for a minute.

Would you give me another shot on Sunday? If I promise I won't go to work, even if no one shows up?

That's easy.

Of course. I would love it. I had a really great time in church with him. I know that sounds weird, but it's true. It was enough.

I type, **Thank you. I look forward to doing it again.**

Church has never been "fun" before. I look forward to seeing you then.

I sigh. I want to see him tonight.

I have to laugh at myself. I'm almost fifty. At my age, it's crazy that I'm mooning over a boy like this.

Not a boy. He's no doubt a man.

Another text comes almost immediately.

I hope you have a good night. I guess you know what I'll be dreaming about.

No. I have no idea what he'll be dreaming about. What in the world makes him think I know?

But I don't say that. Instead, I send something simple.

Good night.

Chapter 22

Tammy

I'm sitting on the porch on Sunday morning. I'm early. As usual.

But the weather has taken a turn, and it's unusually warm.

I know it's not going to last, but I'm sitting outside enjoying it.

I still have probably fifteen minutes until Justin comes, unless he's early. Which wouldn't surprise me. I kind of expect it.

I'm thinking about him and anticipating having a really great day when the fire alarm goes off.

As I always do as soon as I hear the siren, I say a prayer. Not just for whoever it's for, but for the men and women—including my mom—who will be going out to help with whatever happened.

Most likely, it's probably not a fire.

I guess it's a car accident. But I won't know until later.

Mom will tell us about it.

I bet it's less than five minutes later when the fire truck, lights flashing and siren blasting, rolls by my house. Mom, with her snow-white hair a dead giveaway, sits in the driver seat, taking it down the road.

I shake my head a little, but I'm so proud of my mom.

She's a really wonderful woman.

I wish I had half of her bravery.

I've a toe on the porch floor, gently pushing the swing. Not really thinking about anything when Justin pulls in.

I stay where I'm at, confident he saw me. Sure enough, he parks his truck, and Roy and he walk over.

I get up to greet him, and I'm surprised to see he's carrying a box.

It's not wrapped, just plain brown, but I'm surprised nonetheless.

A gift?

Maybe not a gift exactly. Probably he would have wrapped that.

"Good morning," he says, and he's not even using that tone that sends shivers down my spine, yet still, shivers go down my spine.

I'm worse than a teenager.

"Good morning," I say, looking at Justin first and then Roy.

Roy looks cute in a button-down, jeans, and cowboy boots. It's a step up from last week when he wore a T-shirt. His jeans look clean too.

I bite a smile back. Interest in a girl will do that to a man.

I think it's cute.

Justin looks better to me. He's not whipcord thin like his son is, but he's wearing clean jeans and boots, along with the blue plaid button-down that does a whole lot for his eyes.

Or maybe it's just because they're looking at me like he admires me.

I know that's it. I don't give a flip what his eyes look like. Or the rest of him to be honest.

I'm more interested in how he treats me. I like his confidence too. Not cocky, but it's close. Confidence looks good on a man.

I suppose it looks good on a woman too, but I don't really pay attention to that.

I like that he's smiling, in a good mood, and he's on time.

There's something to be said for a man who does what he says he's going to do.

Funny all the things I thought were so important when I was younger—long legs, slim hips, broad shoulders, and a square jaw—I don't care about anymore.

None of it.

I guess a messy divorce will do that to a woman.

Make her wiser.

"I brought something for you." He looks a little sheepish. "I'm sorry I didn't wrap it. I never even thought about wrapping paper until I got home and realized we didn't have any. So I guess you get to open a brown box."

He hands it out, and under the confidence is an insecurity that's endearing. I like that he is concerned that I'm not going to like receiving a box that's not wrapped.

I don't hesitate to put him at ease. "I don't care about the wrapping."

It strikes me that it's true. About men *and* gifts. It's what's inside that counts. Of course.

"You're smiling. What's that for? Are you laughing at the fact that I don't have wrapping paper?"

I shake my head, wondering if I can tell him what I actually was thinking.

Why not?

"I was just thinking that I think about this gift the way I think about men. I don't care what the outside looks like. It's what's inside that counts." It sounds cheesy, but it is so very, very true.

He grins, knowing right away that I am serious, then jerks his head. "Go ahead. Open it."

My eyes shift to Roy, who's got a grin on his face too. I know this isn't going to be a gag gift. At least, I'm like ninety percent sure. I don't think we've been going out long enough for him to goof off with me quite like that.

But this is the guy that ran his remote-control truck into my foot, so...I look up at him. "Is this a remote-control truck?"

"I had no idea you wanted one."

I didn't until this second. But then I think that it actually might be kind of fun. Especially if I had a place like his big store to run it.

"I only want one of those if I can sit in your office above the store and run it like you do."

"You come down to the store after school some night this week, and I'll let you run my remote-control truck." He says it with a grin and humor in his voice, and we share a smile. I think we're both thinking that I'm going to look pretty funny doing that, because I'm just not the kind of person that looks like they're going to enjoy running a remote-control vehicle anywhere, but maybe I'm loosening up a little.

"You have your hair down," he says.

I nod. It's a new look for me. I typically pin it back up out of my face somehow. It gets in the way when I'm teaching, and I also don't like it to fly around.

But Kori had given me a trim at our girls' night—she was a beautician for a while—and it is too short to pin it the way I usually do.

"I like it," he says, and I feel my cheeks heat. I hoped he would.

I set the box on the little table I have on my porch, and I open the flaps. I peer in and gasp. "Oh my goodness! I thought I should get one, then I forgot all about it." I reach in and pull out a helmet. It's the same color as my four-wheeler. I love that detail, that he did that, obviously on purpose.

"I didn't have one that color in the shop so had to special order it. I made an educated guess on the size. Try it on and see if it fits."

"I didn't know there were different-sized helmets."

"Yeah. Nothing too fancy, just small, medium, large, and extra-large. There are some kid sizes too. I've been doing it long enough, I can kinda eyeball it up." He pauses, then he says, "It wasn't a hardship to eyeball you up."

That sounded a little weird, but I laugh because I know what he means and that he means it as a compliment. I take it that way. I think it's dumb to search for things to get offended over. Although I know people who do it.

I don't want to live my life in a constant state of anger and offense.

It slips on and fits perfectly. Snug but not too tight.

I turn with a little flourish, and my eyebrows are lifted. "What do you think?"

"I think I like looking at you better when it's off, but looks like it fits, and you look good in it."

Goodness, the man is full of compliments today.

I pull it off and shake my hair a little. Its style is simple, and I'm pretty sure the helmet didn't mess it up. But even if it did, I think Justin's going to look at me the same, like he admires me. A look that holds affection and humor. A look I'm really starting to love.

"Thank you. Thank you for the compliment. Thank you for the helmet. It was...very considerate." He doesn't seem like the kind of man who would bring me a gift, let alone a thoughtful one like this.

I know a helmet isn't exactly a romantic gift, but the fact that he got it in a color to match my four-wheeler really touches my heart.

I already think he's pretty wonderful, and this is making it harder to resist him.

I'm not sure I even want to anymore.

We walk to church, and it's almost exactly the same as last week. Mrs. Riley meets us again and extols my virtues to Justin.

Justin waits until she takes a breath, and he says, "I think, Mrs. Riley, that you need to start singing my praises to the lady. I'm already sold."

I'm not sure exactly what he means by that, but it makes my heart feel happy.

Mrs. Riley is a little stunned, and she doesn't quite recover before we get to church.

We spend the afternoon riding four-wheelers at his house. I think he's kind of impressed with what I've learned.

I make sure to tell him Roy is an excellent teacher.

Roy has also become an excellent student. Not perfect, C level maybe, but that's a lot better than he was.

He'll be turning his term paper in. I've seen parts of it, and I know it's good; I'm excited for him.

We spend Sunday evening chatting with his neighbor and admiring the daffodils he planted for her.

He makes a small fire in the backyard, and we roast hot dogs and marshmallows over it.

The only thing that would have made the day any more perfect would have been if he kissed me when he dropped me off at my house and opened my door.

He refused my offer to come in for a bit—it truly was late. All he said was, "Good night."

I walk in, happy, glowing, but also disappointed.

My glow evaporates though when I get a text from my sister Claire.

Rachel, from the basketball team, was involved in the accident today. She's in the ICU.

I say another prayer. This one specifically for Rachel, and I also pray for Claire, because I know she loves her girls. I had Rachel in school, and she was a good student. By the time I've had them a whole year, they feel like my own kids. This hits me hard.

We're a small town, and I know there will be fundraisers going on if the family needs it. I'm determined to help as much as I can.

Chapter 23

Justin

I have a good week, although I don't get to spend as much time with Tammy as I want.

She never does make it to the shop to run my remote-control truck.

I'm not sure if she was kidding about that or not.

I kinda think she was. But, on the other hand, she does seem to be loosening up a bit. Which I like, but I like the buttoned-up Tammy, too.

I guess maybe I just like what's inside.

She spends a lot of time this week tutoring someone else after school who is having some trouble in one of her classes. Also, apparently a former student and basketball player was in an accident.

She and her sisters are doing some things with the fire company and the community for that. The last I heard, the girl is going to get better, but her family is facing a lot of medical bills. Not to mention her parents are off work, because the biggest hospital is quite a drive away. I don't know anyone who can live without an income for any length of time.

I am certainly keeping my ear to the ground to see what I can do.

Still, that doesn't overshadow my excitement for Saturday morning.

I pick Tammy up, and she looks fantastic.

Her cheeks are rosy and her eyes are glowing, and I think maybe for the first time, she greets me with a huge smile. She might have thrown her arms around me and given me a hug too, but I reach out to take her hand.

I had been hoping that she'd ask me to kiss her.

So far that strategy hasn't worked, and I'm just looking for an opportunity.

It's not something I'm going to get right now, though, as we pull into the charity run.

We go over to the makeshift table to sign up and pay the entry fees.

It's in a little shed, protected from the rain and sun, and there's a big board behind the table, with the names of the options for the charity donation.

Tammy gasps beside me, and I look to see that she's staring at the board.

I turn to look and run my eyes down over the names.

I recognize some of them. I'm learning the people in the community, and since it's not that big, I hear a lot of what's going on with being in the shop.

Women always get the rap for gossiping, but in my experience, men are worse.

"What?" I ask, when I don't see any names that ring any huge bell that should cause her to gasp.

"Rachel's name is on the list."

I look back, and sure enough, there's a Rachel up there.

"It's the basketball player?"

She nods. "Yes."

She told me that she was a former student as well, and I know Tammy has taken it hard. She loves her students. I witnessed this firsthand as I've seen the lengths that she's gone through to help my son, not just to keep him from failing but to help him actually learn.

I know the techniques that she's taught him will help him be able to write when he needs to. He's also taking typing from an older student during a study hall.

He won't get any credit for it, but it's a necessary skill to have. I'm glad she made sure he got the opportunity.

"I wasn't caring how I did in the race, but I sure hope whoever wins the money chooses Rachel."

I don't say anything, because I know it's not a guarantee. Some of those names are up there because they're relatives of people who regularly participate.

The regular participants have sway in getting names suggested.

They also have an advantage, because they know the track, and the more a person runs it, the better you get, like anything else.

"Have you ever won?" she asks in a low voice, looking at me.

"I've never actually come in first." I lift my shoulder, a little grin on my face. "I know men are supposed to be really competitive and live to win, but when I get out there, I usually just enjoy the scenery, and love being in the woods, and appreciate the ride. A couple of times, I've stopped at the river we cross and just hung out there for a while."

I almost feel like I'm getting sappy, and I don't mean to. But I do like being out. I don't do this to race as fast as I can, because I figure it's just over faster that way.

Sometimes when Roy has gone with me, we've gone fishing for a while. There's also a nice overlook.

Speaking of Roy, he's back at the school, playing basketball, which has almost become his life.

I guess kids grow up and stop doing so much with their parents, and I'm okay with that, but it does make me a little sad. Especially since I missed so much of his early life.

"I like that," she says, and I kind of have it in the back of my mind that I'd like to take her to the overlook and maybe hang out at the river.

"So, if you win today, you'll choose Rachel?" she asks, looking hopeful and sweet.

It's funny, even though she's dressed almost like the rest of the folks here, she still sticks out. She just has a classy look to her, maybe the way she holds herself, that draws attention. Not that she looks stuck up or anything, just well put together. Tidy almost.

I like it, but I think I'd like the way she looked even if it were different. She'd still be Tammy, no matter what she wears or how she looks, and that's what I like.

"Sure. I wasn't planning on trying to win, though. I figured I'd ride with you."

She bites her lip, but before she can say any more, the people in front of us walk away, and it is our turn to register.

These rides are really popular and draw people from all over. A lot of times, purses are pretty large, and I get to thinking about what Tammy has said.

I know Rachel means a lot to her and her family, and there is no guarantee that the person who wins will pick her.

There is also no guarantee that her name will be on the list again. There are always families who need help.

We have a good thirty minutes before it's time to start. After we register and get our machines unloaded, I take her hand and walk down to the starting line.

"The people who are racing to win will crowd the line first. I figure you and I will hang back and let everyone go."

"Then you're riding with me?" she asks, and she says it kind of low.

"I don't want you to go by yourself your first time. Not that there's any danger, and not that the trail isn't well marked, I just feel like it'd be rude to ditch you."

"Would it be ditching me if I ask you to try to win?"

I grin. "If you're not careful, I'm going to start thinking you don't want to ride with me."

"I just know Rachel's family can use all the help that they can get. And while I know that there will be plenty of other opportunities and fundraisers, I'd just like to do what we can for her." She lifts a slender shoulder. She's actually wearing a sweatshirt. It's the first time I've seen her in one. It has a hood. I know there's a slender body under there, but it's bulky enough that you really can't tell. It'll keep her warm. I'm not entirely sure, but I think she has a vest on under it.

I know she'll be fine.

"So you're saying you'd rather I race to win, and you'd rather ride by yourself?" I ask, just to be sure.

She nods. I look at the starting line, and I think to myself what all winning will entail.

I'm probably just as skilled as anyone else riding in the race today, although my machine might be slightly older...which gives me an idea.

I turned to her. "Let me ride your machine. It's got more power than mine. I can't guarantee I'll win. I've never actually tried, but I'll do my best. Of course, I can't help what chips I get."

"I think it's worth a try. And of course, you can ride my machine. I'm sure you'll do better on it than I will anyway." There she is, biting her lip again. "Will I be able to ride yours?"

"Sure. You run it the exact same way you run yours."

She nods. She's seen me run it, although she's never actually driven it herself.

I feel like this is a bad idea. I don't want to leave her by herself.

There are a few other women here, but it's mostly men. I don't think anyone would do anything, or that she would be in any danger, I just feel like it's my responsibility to protect her. I can't do that if I'm racing at the front.

But I can't tell her no, either.

It's settled, and I stand at the line and try to explain to her everything she'll need to do.

She accuses me of being a mother hen.

Her accusation is fair. Because I am.

Chapter 24

Tammy

I know Justin doesn't want to leave me to ride alone. He has no idea how much that means to me, that he was going to make sure he was with me throughout my first run. I honestly hadn't been sure.

I think it means just as much to me, maybe more, that he's willing to not do what he wants to do and to do what I asked him to. I really care about Rachel, and I know her family seriously needs this money.

But it's kind of funny how by not riding with me, he just pushed me that much closer to falling in love with him. I don't know if that's his goal or not, but if it is, it's working.

Maybe I should say, it's worked.

I've never seen this many four-wheelers in one place. Of course, that's not exactly surprising, considering I've only been riding two weeks.

He said the trail is well marked, and I'm not scared, but it does make me nervous to be riding around so many other people.

I actually feel very comfortable on my four-wheeler. It's very much like driving a car and not nearly as difficult as I thought it would be.

I am getting pretty good at riding on Justin's trails if I do say so my-self. Not race worthy or anything like that, but I seem to have a knack for it. Which is odd.

I also have a little bit of a lead foot.

Maybe I should say, lead thumb, since the throttle is a lever I work with my thumb.

People line up, and like Justin said, the serious guys are in front. He's there, too.

I suddenly realize this could be dangerous.

Normally, that's the first thing I think about, but for some reason, it slipped my mind. I guess I was too focused on Rachel and hoping that she would win the cash donation.

Being that this is the first run of the year, Justin explained that several businesses, including his, have pledged to match whatever the pot is, so it's actually a pot that will be almost ten times bigger than it normally is.

That's quite a lot of money, and Rachel's family can use it.

The gun goes off, and despite the large amount of money, I wish with all my heart I wouldn't have asked Justin to do what I did.

If I had seen this one time, I never would have. The ATVs are so close together there's barely any space between them.

I hardly think that when two machines get their tires mixed up, and somehow, they both end up flipping onto their sides.

I don't think either of the riders are hurt, because they both get up, but it scares me. If I had any way of communicating with Justin, I would ask him to forget it. But he's almost out of sight. Even though I can only see the back of the machines, my blue one stands out.

I offered to let him use my helmet, but he gently declined and kept his black one.

The blue one I'm wearing, the one he got me, doesn't go too bad with his black machine, but it looks better with mine.

The next wave of people leave, just like Justin said they would.

These are the people that are hoping that none of the front-runners get five chips in a row, and they might be able to be the first to do that, even though they're not planning on winning the race.

I almost leave with this group. If I had ever done this before, I might have.

I feel like my skills are satisfactory, and I might be able to run with them, but I promised Justin I wouldn't.

They leave, and there are a few of us left. Some older men and a few couples that must be doing this as a date type thing.

Which isn't a bad idea. The way Justin had talked, and the way he'd looked, I think that was what he had in mind.

I'm not sure I can make it up to him.

Other than committing to coming again.

I'm at the front of this last pack, which is really not much of an accomplishment. But it feels like it is, and I let myself smile about it.

Justin said it would probably take me about two hours, if I ride at a nice, slow, steady pace.

He told me to make sure that I stop and pick up chips at every station. He said it's never happened that no one has gotten five in a row, but he did say a couple of times no one in the front two groups got it.

I do what he says, and as I'm driving, I definitely wish that he was with me. There's some woods, and though I am not afraid, I am a little nervous.

I guess I can outrun any animal on this, but I really don't want to have to try.

There are a couple places where it's muddy.

Justin had said there might be spots like that, and he'd shown me how to put it in four-wheel drive.

I use that twice.

I've been riding for about thirty minutes, and I've gotten pretty confident in my abilities, and maybe I am going a little faster than I should have been. I go around a bend in the trail, and no one who knows me would actually believe this, but I lean in the turn and kind of gun it, swinging the rear end around and flinging mud back.

You would not believe how fun this is.

I come swinging around the corner, and there's a lake in front of me. The trail goes right through it, and I would not have, except I was going too fast to stop.

Maybe I should rephrase. I was going too fast to stop before I got into the lake.

It's not really a lake but a big mud puddle. It looks like a lake since it is spread all over both sides of the trail.

I can see tire tracks where the people ahead of me had gone around it. That seems like the smart thing to do, but I am almost at the middle of it before I get myself stopped.

I think I should probably just keep going through, because to sit might be to sink.

The water is up to the footrest, but it's not getting any deeper, so I go forward after putting it in four-wheel-drive.

I'm almost out, only maybe ten feet left, when the mud gets deeper, and the water covers the footrest.

I admit I panic a little and gun the motor.

Probably not the smartest thing I ever did.

Muddy water flies everywhere, and my machine weaves back and forth. At least I'm going forward and am not stuck.

At the end of the mud puddle, there's deep mud, but I'm going fast enough that I fly through it as globs of mud shoot through the air, landing on me and my helmet and Justin's machine.

I can't see a thing now because my helmet is covered in mud, so I put the face shield up before I keep going.

Going through that lake and actually making it, and then making it through the mud on the other side has given me confidence.

I finish the course in ninety minutes, thirty minutes faster than Justin had suggested I would.

I admit I am covered, absolutely covered, in mud, from my helmet, to my face, to my entire body.

I'm wet and a little cold, but I am also crazy happy and almost bubbling over with this excited, confident feeling of accomplishment.

It wasn't something that I expected to feel, and I can't keep the grin off my face.

Justin is waiting for me, and I think his smile matches mine.

I'm not sure which one of us is filthier, because he's covered in just as much mud as I am.

I look around for my machine, but they're all mud brown, and I have no idea which one it is.

I've barely crossed the finish line when he comes running toward me. I park and get off and meet him with my arms out.

I guess I don't really mean to give him a hug, but that's exactly what happens, and I think we're just both excited.

I think his excitement is because he sees me, which really makes me feel good.

I ask, "How'd you do?" I'm thinking about the money and Rachel, and I'm shocked when he says, "I won."

But then his face falls some, and he says, "But I didn't get the right chips."

Then his eyes drop again. "No one did."

I'm excited that he won, disappointed that his chips didn't line up, but I'm eager to try mine. We're also grinning at each other, and he says, "I can't believe you made it. Did you see that huge mud puddle?"

"Of course. The one that looked like a lake?"

"Yeah. I almost went through it. I was really trucking around that turn."

"I actually did go through it. I was trucking around the turn too," I say, and he smiles, although there's disbelief on his face.

"Really? You're serious?"

I nod, loving the look in his eyes.

"I can't believe it. I thought that was deep. I figured I'd end up swimming if I went through. I can't believe you did."

"I didn't mean to. I was going too fast to stop."

He laughs, loud and full, and I laugh with him. I can't remember the last time I've enjoyed laughing with someone so much.

He's still shaking his head, his arms around me, as he looks into my eyes and says, "I just can't believe it. You are something else."

"I had fun. Honest. I was not expecting to enjoy it as much as I did." My lips pull back a little. "It would have been better if you had been with me."

"For me too. I've never won before, but I didn't need to and I don't care to do it again. I'd rather be with you."

His face has gotten serious, and I don't know whether he tugged me, or I just did it on my own, but I step closer, and my arms go around his shoulders again, and my fingers brush his neck.

His breathing changes, and so does my heartbeat. It can't decide whether it wants to go fast or lopsided, but it feels like it is taking a corner on two wheels, which feels good but scary at the same time.

"I guess you know by now that I'm crazy for you," he says, and that does nothing to steady my heart. If anything, it's upside down now.

Chapter 25

Tammy

"We're so different." I say, and then I have to laugh a little. "Maybe not." I think of the mud that covers me, and how much fun I had today, and how much I enjoy being with him. How he can make me laugh, and he teases me out of my serious moods.

He's sweet and funny and kind, and yet he's all man, and I realize, "Never mind. I think I just realized you're perfect. For me."

"The lady's a little slow on the uptake. I recognized the second you walked into my shop, and my truck landed on your toe, that you were perfect for me."

"No, you didn't. You hated me." I know he can't be serious.

"I can't say I fell in love at that second, but I can say I fell in intrigue at that second. The feeling hasn't left."

I know this is not the place to have a romantic conversation, but even though there are still people crossing the finish line and a few people milling around, most people have either loaded up their machines and left or are in the process of doing so.

No one is paying any attention to us, not that I care.

"I think I believe you."

"You'd better. It's the truth." His finger runs over my brow, brushing a piece of mud off, and then it goes down my face, a light touch, but just a little rough, with the calluses on his thumb.

It feels perfect.

"You have so many layers, every time I'm with you, you surprise me with something new." His voice is still low, and somehow, his words make my mouth dry.

"I guess the real me is down there somewhere," I say, knowing that he isn't exactly complaining, but he could have been.

156

"I think they're all a part of you. I know it's not romantic to compare you to an onion, but every layer that you peel off an onion is still part of the onion."

The man can make me smile, even when he's holding me and saying all the sweet words. All the mostly sweet words.

"An onion?"

"I never said I was romantic. After all, a helmet doesn't exactly scream romance."

"It's romantic to come to the firehouse and buy flowers from me. It's romantic to be on time and to be there when you say you're going to be. It's romantic to open my door and to make sure I have a helmet." I know I'm taking a chance here, but after the day I had, I have the confidence to do it. "It's romantic to look at me when I'm covered in mud, like I'm the most beautiful woman in the world. It's romantic that you have the confidence in me that I could do this today. It's romantic that you're tender and sweet and funny and you always make me smile. I think you're romantic and you don't even know it."

"I thought romance meant roses and candy, and I haven't even thought about that."

"Don't. You're perfectly romantic just the way you are," I say, and I mean it.

"I noticed that you didn't say it was romantic that I haven't kissed you."

There my lips go up again. That man.

"That's because it's not," I say, and I don't even have to gather any nerve to do it.

"I feel like I need to fix that."

"The sooner, the better."

His lips lower, and this is one time I'm happy I'm tall. It doesn't take any time at all for them to meet mine, and all those romantic things he did don't compare to the romance in that man's kiss.

He's deadly romantic when he can make me forget that I'm standing out in front of God and everybody, and I'm covered in mud, and I'm wet and cold.

I'm not cold anymore.

I'm not the one who pulls away first, either. I have to say that because it's true.

He leans his forehead against mine, and his breath fans my face. "You always surprise me."

"I don't know why you stopped." In the back of my head, I can't believe I say that. I can't believe I actually feel that way.

But it's true. I definitely didn't want him to.

"I said I was crazy about you," he says, and his eyes are closed.

"Yes?" I murmur, just loving standing in his arms.

"I guess I can tell you the truth now."

"The truth?" He startles me some with this. I'm a little scared. My stomach turns in on itself.

"Yeah. The truth. I'm not just a little crazy about you. I love you. All of you. All the layers." That smile I love tilts up one side of his mouth. "I definitely love the way you kiss. Pretty amazing."

Okay. I have to admit no one has ever said anything like this to me before, and it feels good. Being with Justin feels good.

"I've fallen in love with you too. A while ago. But especially when I asked you to try to win, and even though you didn't want to, you did. And the reason you didn't want to was because you wanted to be with me. I love both of those things."

"I'm not messing around with this. I mean, I'm serious about you. I'm not asking you to marry me right now, but that's what I'm planning on." His eyes open. He holds my gaze with his. "I just want to make sure I'm clear about what I want."

It is my turn to close my eyes and take a deep breath. The M word scares me. I didn't have a good experience. I lost everything. Everything that meant anything to me is gone. Sure, I chat on Snapchat with my boys and FaceTime them, but I lost my family, I lost my home, and I was a mess for a long time.

"I'm scared," I finally say.

He grunts. "I can't believe you drove through that lake, and you're scared of me."

"Not you. I'm scared to lose everything again. It hurts."

"I know."

And I realize he does. He knows just as well as I do. Because he lost everything too.

Of course, Roy is back with him now, but he hadn't been.

"You do. You do know." I swallow. "What you want is what I want, but I'm afraid to have."

"Do you think you'll ever be unafraid?" he asks, and the hope in his voice is muted, but it's there.

"I do. Maybe not with anyone but you." I feel like I can take a chance on him.

That statement makes his mouth curve. "As long as there's a chance, I'm willing to wait. However long it takes. As long as I know that it's just you and me and no one else, we can just take it easy, and whenever you're ready, you can let me know. Know that I am, and I'm just waiting on you."

That is more than fair. I appreciate it. After all, it's been a whirlwind time.

I nod. "Thank you."

"This waiting, though, it includes kissing, right?"

I grin. He loves looking at me, he loves being with me, and he loves kissing me. What else could a girl want?

"Maybe you'd better kiss me again before we come to a firm decision on that," I say, and although he knows I'm joking, he does exactly what I want him to do.

This one is even better than the first, but it is shorter, because we are interrupted.

"Hey, you two? Everyone's tried their chips, except you." The man who'd been watching people as they came in and tried their chips on the board points at me. I vaguely realize this, but I'm still a little dazed by Justin's kiss.

I think we're both a little dazed, because it takes a bit before either one of us completely pulls apart and realizes we need to follow the guy to the shed.

I get my chips out and try to match up the colors. I'm dirty, the chips are dirty, and there's about fifty people trying to look over my shoulder. Everyone wants to see someone win.

I get four in a row, and my hands are shaking as I hold the last three chips.

I almost cry when none of the rest of them provide the fifth chip to win.

The man standing on the other side, supervising, says, "You won't believe this, but you're the first person to get four." His lips flatten and turn down. "But that's not enough."

"They must have made it a little harder this year. This isn't quite the way the board was laid out before," Justin says, studying the squares.

"They added more colors. I might suggest we go back to the original. It will be terrible if no one wins."

I almost turn away when Mrs. Pinkerton, the high school principal, looks up from where she is counting the money.

I hadn't seen her when we signed in earlier and didn't realize she was part of these charity runs.

I suppose my mouth is hanging open. It must look ridiculous too, since that is the only part of me that doesn't have mud caked on it.

"Tamera?" Mrs. Pinkerton says, peering at me, like she isn't sure or, more likely, can't believe it is me.

I'm sure I don't look like myself.

To say the least.

"My goodness, Tamera, that *is* you." Her eyes move to Justin. "Are you with Mr. Gabriel?" she asks, then shakes her head. "I would never have guessed."

Then, to my horror, she whips out her phone. "Give me a smile. Every teacher that goes through gets her picture taken and put in the school newsletter."

I recall vaguely seeing something to that effect in the school newsletter. But it always kind of horrified me that people had allowed their pictures to be taken when they look so terrible.

But she's the principal, and while she isn't the final say about whether or not I have a job, she reports to people who do, so I smile.

Maybe I should say I grimace.

Regardless, she snaps the picture, and while not getting the money to go to Rachel has put a damper on my enthusiasm, I'm still pretty psyched.

"Thanks so much, Tamera. I'll go ahead and give this to the church so they can use it in their newsletter as well. I'm sure you're proud of yourself."

Wonderful. I'm not really embarrassed at what I've done, but I don't usually go out in public looking like this.

"No one is going to notice the mud. All they're going to see is your beautiful smile," Justin says, and he puts his arm around me.

I look up at him, knowing that's not true but loving that he says it anyway.

"You want to leave? You want to hang around and see if someone wins?" he asks.

Several people crossed the finish line while we were in the shed, and one person is standing beside us, trying to line up their chips.

I really want to stay and see who the charity pot goes to, but I figure Justin probably has better things to do. He's already spent the day doing what I wanted instead of what he wanted.

So I ask, "What do you want?"

"I don't mind staying. But I guess I'd rather go home and get cleaned up." He shifts his weight and puts a hand in his pocket. "But either way, I was kind of hoping to spend the rest of the day with you."

He does look hopeful. My smile gets bigger.

"Then let's do that. We'll go home and get cleaned up, and I suppose we ought to clean our machines too. How do you do that anyway?" I have visions of running them through the car wash. But that wouldn't work.

"A hose and elbow grease. Might want to do that before we clean ourselves," he says. "Sometimes, it can get a little messy." His look turns thoughtful. "Actually, if you're not planning on riding yours, I can drop them both off at the shop. I'll just do it tomorrow while I'm at work. What do you think of that?"

I'm cold. I'm wet and muddy, and that sounds really good to me. I tell him so, and we start walking toward our machines to drive them to the truck and trailer and get them loaded.

It's crazy, but I'm actually able to help him get everything loaded and strapped down. As far as I know, no one has won when we pull out.

Chapter 26

Justin

We've showered, gotten cleaned up, picked my son up at the school, and now we're all at my house. I feel like I'm the luckiest man in the world.

Tammy is curled up on the couch with me, snuggled in my arms, and I have to say, she fits perfectly.

I could stay like this forever. I am not sure what I did to deserve it, but I'm grateful.

I'm also confident.

I know this is new, and I know she's been hurt, and I can respect that. But I know she'll come around.

A woman like Tammy isn't going to kiss me and let me hold her like this, if she's not thinking long term. Especially when she knows I am.

I can't wait to take her out in the woods.

I'm guessing she might not like it, but I think it'll grow on her.

And if it doesn't, I'd rather give up the woods than Tammy.

My phone rings, and Tammy stirs.

My son, who is sitting out at the kitchen table doing his schoolwork, looks up. He's in my line of sight from where I'm reclining on the couch. I reach over and grab my phone that's sitting on the coffee table beside Tammy's.

She shifts, and I tighten my arm around her, not wanting her to move.

"Please stay," I say.

She relaxes, and so do I.

Using one hand, I swipe my phone and put it on speaker. I kinda feel like it'd be rude for me to have a conversation with someone else while I'm holding the woman I love, but maybe it's not quite as rude if she can hear it too.

"Hello?"

"Justin. I'm glad I caught you. It's Marshall, from the charity run."

I recognize him. We're not great friends, but he's the man who organizes everything and is in charge. He owns the grounds, too.

"What can I do for you?" I figure it probably has something to do with my business and soliciting donations or something.

I've talked to him about those things before, and my business is pretty heavily involved in it. A lot of the people who do the charity runs are my customers. I get a little advertising out of it.

"I'm calling because we never ended up with a winner. First time it's ever happened. So, I got together with the rest of the organizers, and we decided rather than waiting until the next run, we'd have you choose your charity, since you won the race."

Tammy tenses in my arms, and I know that this has just thrilled her, and I'm thrilled for her. It also makes me feel better about leaving her to run by herself while I ran with the front. It kinda makes it worthwhile.

"I choose Rachel. The high school girl who played basketball and is in ICU."

"She's actually out of the ICU. But great. I was kinda pulling for her too. Her family can definitely use it."

"Yeah. That's what I've heard. Good to hear she's out."

"It's going to be a long road for her, but she's gonna make it, and the money will most certainly help. Sorry to bother you. Thanks a lot."

We hang up, and immediately Tammy rolls until she's facing me, and she takes my cheeks in her hands.

Love that smile. It makes me happy. Beyond happy, to know that I am the reason it's there.

"Thank you. Thank you so much."

That's all she says, but it's all she needs to say. Actually, she doesn't even need to say that, but I can hear everything she feels in her voice.

If that weren't enough, she punctuates it with a kiss, and I'm sorry, but that woman is one hen of the kisser.

And that's all I'm going to say about that.

Chapter 27

Tammy

I am sitting on a cliff at some crazy early hour in the morning, Justin's legs bent on either side of my body and his torso against my back. He has his arms around me and his head next to mine. We're both staring at the sunrise.

Birds chirp around us. I can hear a stream tripping over rocks in the distance, and, in one of the three tents that are set up behind us, Roy is snoring.

"Don't you think we should wake him up? He's missing some of the most beautiful sky I've ever seen," I say in a soft voice that isn't quite a whisper.

"Nah. Someday he'll have a woman of his own to share this with. Somehow that makes getting up a lot easier."

I can hear the humor in Justin's voice. I love that he always seems to be laughing at the world. I also love that he only has eyes for me.

Well, and the sunset.

He wants to spend every second he can with me. Even if that means he lies on the couch and stares at me while I correct papers.

I suppose some people would hate that, but after what I've been through, I appreciate having someone who actually wants me. Really wants me.

The sky is a deep velvet blue above us with flaming orange along the tops of the distant mountains. Pinks and light blue expand beyond that until they disappear into the deep darkness above us.

The early morning Idaho sky is so beautiful it hurts my heart – in the very best way – to look at it.

"Do you think Roy will be okay with my parents?" I ask.

His arms tighten around me. I know he loves his son and had hoped Roy would want to go with us. We're going to see my ex – which makes my stomach hurt and I appreciate the comfort of Justin's arms – and my boys, which, of course, makes every pain in my stomach worth it.

Justin insisted as soon as school was out that we needed to go and spend at least a week.

He wants to spend every other week this summer with my ex and my boys.

I don't think I could stand the insults and put downs, except with Justin behind me, I know I can.

Justin is convinced that if we spend enough time there, my ex might not get sick of us, but his wife surely will. Justin thinks we'll get the custody arrangement changed from unlimited visits for me to shared time, which is what it should have been to begin with.

I'm not as confident, but I'm dying to see my boys. If that means I have to be uncomfortable in the presence of my ex, so be it. Again, with Justin, I think I can handle it.

"I think this is the way it's supposed to be," he says in my ear.

"Starting the day looking at the sunrise?" I say, thinking I know what he means.

"That too," he kind of chuckles. "But also just having another person to walk this life beside you. Someone who feels like your missing half. Someone who makes you feel like they're the piece that makes your life complete."

I know what he means but his words scare me, too. I know what it feels like when the piece that makes your life complete leaves. It feels like part of you has been ripped off and you have to live life with the pain of an open, gaping hole in yourself – a hole and pain that no one else can see.

But Justin feels as steady as the rock beneath us. He's latched onto me and has somehow found things to admire and respect and love and has made me want to reach out again – to open myself, not just to him, but to the possibility of allowing someone to be my other half and de-pending on them to complete me.

More than that, I want to be that for him – to love him the way a man like him deserves and to be the partner he needs.

"How do you feel about getting married before we leave?" I hold myself very still as I whisper these words. Even though I know this is what I want, there is still a part of me that is afraid.

I want to open my arms and embrace the fear. I can't have what I want if I walk away from the chances life offers me.

I can't be the person I was meant to be alone.

I need Justin.

His arms tighten and I don't have to hear the joy in his tone to know I've made him very happy. How does making someone else happy increase my own joy beyond words?

"I want that," he says simply. "But only if you're sure."

He doesn't ask about a wedding, because he knows how hard an-other marriage will be for me. I don't want to have to stand up in front of people and make an even bigger deal about it. I'm scared enough.

I'm so thankful he understands.

"I'm sure," I say, and I know that's true. Confidence in the right path does not mean lack of fear. It just means that I'm not going to let my fear keep me from walking where I know I'm meant to. With whom I'm meant to.

"Tomorrow?" he asks.

The sky has exploded in color and blazing glory. Maybe it's a good omen, or maybe it's just Idaho.

Regardless, my word is sure. "Yes. Tomorrow. Would you marry me tomorrow?"

I can feel his smile against my cheek. I'm not the kind of woman who asks a man to marry me. And he is the kind of man who would be begging me to do so. The fact that he's given me this time to work things out in my head, and the fact that I'm so sure I asked him, means we're both completely invested.

Our opposite natures balance each other out perfectly, and Justin is the kind of man who will stand beside me forever, no matter what.

I hope he knows that's the kind of woman I am.

"Do you mind spending our honeymoon with my ex and boys?"

"And you. I'll spend it with anyone as long as you're there, too."

I knew that's what he would say.

The glory of the sunrise is fading now and I'm starting to feel the cold, hard ground under my butt. Not that I have any desire to move. Wherever Justin is is where I want to be.

"You about ready to go cook breakfast with me," he asks.

I nod.

"Do you think I might be able to go first today?" he asks, and the humor is back in his tone.

He had a good time teasing me about how fast I drove yesterday. I admit, I love speed. I know I don't look like the type, but it's true.

"As long as I get to lead tomorrow," I tease. We're spending three days in the woods, riding our ATVs with Justin showing Roy and me some of his favorite places in the Idaho Rockies. Like this one – where we've watched the sunrise the last two mornings before spending the day on trails, either riding, hiking or hanging out.

I expected to enjoy it, although I know Justin was nervous that I wouldn't. Why not? I'm with him.

And that's all I need.

Epilogue
Leah

I wasn't expecting to attend a wedding today.

My sister Tammy is not exactly a spur-of-the-moment person.

But she came back from the woods with her boyfriend, Justin, and his son Roy and announced that they were getting married.

Today.

Tonight, actually.

That was a little over an hour ago.

Now we're in our parents' house with our pastor standing almost regally beside the threadbare and broken recliner that dad absolutely loves and refuses to part with, with my other two sisters, Claire and Kori, along with Claire's children and her fiancé, Trey.

And our parents, of course.

Tammy is wearing jeans and a sweatshirt.

I think I can count on one hand the number of times I've seen her in a sweatshirt, but I think I understand why.

She was hurt so terribly by her divorce and her ex that she just can't make a big celebration out of this.

I feel a little bad about that, but I also know that just because she's not celebrating, doesn't mean she doesn't mean every single word she's saying.

She'll keep her vows until she dies, and Justin will too.

Despite the sweatshirt, my oldest, regal sister is absolutely glowing.

I'm thrilled that she's so happy.

I'm also a little jealous.

My marriage was pretty much a mistake from the first day, and by the time he left me two years later, it was a relief and I was almost happy to see him go.

I'm not really interested in doing it again. I'm much happier to focus on my job – which I'm not going to have for much longer if I can't convince my boss that the seniors at our assisted living center want to do more than play bingo for the rest of their lives.

I mean, some of them enjoy bingo. I do too on occasion. Strip bingo is actually quite entertaining (ladies who have a top AND a bottom plate to their dentures have a distinct advantage to those of us who don't), but, come on! Everyone wants to do more than play bingo seven nights a week.

I'm going to convince Mr. Ripley of that, just as soon as I've served my reprimand for our last, late night foray into the kitchen where the ladies took the plastic wrap and aluminum foil and made themselves beautiful prom dresses with it.

They were not quite finished with mine when Mr. Ripley came into work at six am (who in the world knew he came into work that early? And why??) and there were parts of me that were still uncovered.

The man acted like he'd never seen a woman's naked big toe before and slapped me with a two week reprimand – after I put my shoes and socks back on (and cut the beautiful half-finished prom dress off and put the rest of my clothes back on as well) and crawled into his office.

Goodness, the man is annoying.

But the ladies and I are never going to get our whitewater rafting trip if I don't crawl and grovel and pretty much figure out how to be nice to that man.

I think it's impossible, but for my ladies, and for the future of our facility and for my job, I'm going to try.

~~~

You can listen to the professionally produced and performed audio of Me and the Tidy Tornado HERE[1] on Say with Jay YouTube channel.

---

1. https://www.youtube.com/watch?v=jyVE-U7JS1I&t=992s

Support our efforts to bring you quality audio at a price that fits into everyone's budget – FREE – check out all the FREE Dyess/Gussman audios HERE[2] **and hit the "Subscribe"** button while you're there. Thanks so much!

Sign up for Jessie's newsletter HERE[3] and find out why readers say, "I eagerly look forward to Tuesday mornings" and "Jessie's newsletter is the only author newsletter that I read every word."

~~~

Enjoy this preview of *Me and the Helpful Hurricane*, just for you!

---

2.   https://www.youtube.com/c/SaywithJay

3.   https://dl.bookfunnel.com/97elto4gwl

Me and the Helpful Hurricane
Chapter 1

Leah

I am in trouble.

So. Much. Trouble.

With my boss.

I guess for those of you who read the books about my sisters, Claire and Tammy, you might be thinking that you're about to read a romance.

I'm sorry, but that's not what you're getting in this book.

My name is Leah Harding. Harding is my maiden name, although I was married for two years. I never changed it.

I guess that's how committed I was to the marriage.

Kids. We were stupid, right?

Anyway, it's been fifteen years, and I have no desire to get married again.

So this book is not going to be a romance.

I'm sorry, but it's probably going to be mostly about me complaining about my insufferable, arrogant, jerk, and—since I'm an honest person, I also need to say—very handsome, very smart, very compassionate boss.

His name is Doug Ripley.

And he is going to kill me when he sees what the ladies at the Cherry Tree Senior Living Center and I have done now.

It's Saturday, and he shouldn't be in, but he thrives on doing the unexpected.

Or maybe I should say he thrives on catching me doing the unexpected and then slapping me with a reprimand.

I'm still under the last reprimand that, if you read Tammy's book, you know about.

173

Just suffice to say, my boss saw more of me than what I was planning on when the ladies at the assisted living center and I spent the entire night in the kitchen using plastic wrap and aluminum foil to make ourselves prom dresses.

Hey, sometimes you just have to make your own fun.

Doug doesn't understand that.

That's what we're doing right now.

"We" as in me and Gertrude, who has salt-and-pepper hair that is naturally curly and cut close to her head. She's in her late 70s, and she's a hoot.

Although the leader, always the leader, of our little group is Agnes, who has snow-white hair and looks like the grandmother in "Little Red Riding Hood."

At least, the way I always picture the granny to look. Kind of old, very sweet—the cookie baking kind of grandmother—except Agnes has a lot of tricks up her sleeve.

She's 80, and she's celebrating her eighth decade on this earth by getting me into as much trouble as she possibly can.

Let me rephrase.

She doesn't want to die without completing all the items on her bucket list.

If you keep reading, you'll hear Agnes talk a lot about her bucket list. It's my job as the activities director at the Cherry Tree Senior Living Center in Good Grief, Idaho, where the ladies are all residents, to provide entertainment and activities.

Agnes is my right-hand lady.

Sometimes, I think she would do my job better than I do. But she's too busy coming up with crazy ideas and plans to actually have a job.

She says now that she's retired—she just retired a couple of years ago in her late seventies, from her job as administrative assistant at a potato-packing factory—that she's busier now than she was when she was working.

I think Agnes is the kind of lady who was always very busy, but hey, I don't argue with her.

Now, I suppose before I tell you why I'm in so much trouble—and why I'm sneaking around with a flower shovel in one hand and a bag of dirt in the other, creeping across the yard of Cherry Tree, right behind Agnes—I should tell you about the third member of our group this evening.

Her name is Harriet, and you won't be able to miss her. Her hair is dyed a bright orange and has been for the last thirty years.

Before that, I think it might have been black, but when it turned gray, she decided she'd always wanted to be a redhead.

Once she chose the color, it turned out bright orange. She decided it gave her verve and made her flashy, and she didn't want to change it.

So, she's the easiest to pick out. Although Agnes's snow-white hair sticks out too.

Regardless, despite being a redhead, or orange head, or whatever you call someone with orange hair, Harriet is the most laid back of the three and most likely to be in the back.

Unless I am.

Most of the time, I'm okay going along with everything we do, but this is kind of pushing things, and I'm already skating on thin ice, as Doug would say. He has a tendency to use old clichés like that, that we might have grown up with back in the olden days of the seventies and eighties.

I assume, although I could be wrong, that he's older than I am, which is pushing forty.

Only when men age, they look good.

His hair is salt-and-pepper, but it makes him look distinguished. My hair, which is still more pepper than salt but is getting to the half-and-half stage, doesn't make me look distinguished. It just makes me look old.

I don't know what Doug looked like when he was younger, but he's getting a little thick around the waist, which, again, doesn't look bad on a man his age.

Me? The thickness I've gained around the waist stands out like flashing neon lights on a nativity scene at Christmastime.

It looks terrible, in other words.

All right, so you already know I have a shovel and a bag of dirt. And I'm crouched down, following Agnes, who also has a shovel and a bag of dirt.

We're dumping the dirt at the far end of Cherry Tree.

I'm not too worried about people inside finding out what we're doing.

First of all, there are only ten total residents, three of whom are outside with me. Of the ones who are still inside, most of them are not going to care. None of them are going to be surprised to see that Agnes and Gertrude and Harriet and I are up to some kind of craziness again.

The facility was built to hold fifty people.

If we don't figure something out to get more people, and fast, it's going to be closing.

Gertrude, Agnes, and Harriet don't want to lose their home. All of them have lived their entire lives in Idaho, and they want to stay here.

I don't want to lose my job. Not because of getting fired, and not because of Cherry Tree closing. The first being more likely than the second today, for me anyway.

But what else do I have to do on a Saturday morning, very, very early, than to work on digging a hole to China?

This is on Agnes's bucket list. (I told you, you were going to be hearing about that.)

All of us know that we are not actually going to get to China, but we're hoping to get a cave big enough at least to hide in.

That's what the ladies said anyway. And I'm all for it.

Well, all for it except I know Doug is going to be extremely upset when he finds out that we've been digging a cave in the beautifully manicured lawn of Cherry Tree.

Now, just so you know that I'm not completely crazy or rude, we're not doing it right in the middle, even though that was the softest spot and we thought it would be the easiest.

We aren't trying to make trouble on purpose, just trying to have some fun, so we decided to dig our hole off to the side where it would be least noticeable.

But we have to put the dirt somewhere, and on the other side the nursing center in the back, there is already some dirt left over from when it was built five years ago. That seemed like the best place—read: "least noticeable" place.

Another truckload of dirt on that pile won't really make a difference, right?

Agnes and I are on a team, and we carry dirt while Gertrude and Harriet dig, putting it in their burlap bags that Harriet, who's late husband also worked at the potato-packing facility south of town, had from way back. Back when they used to use burlap bags.

I'm not sure how she managed to get them into Cherry Tree under the watchful eyes of her children, who helped her move in and made sure that she didn't take more than what would fit in her small, allotted rooms.

But Harriet is one of those people who just seems to have everything you could ever need somewhere on her person or in her possession.

She's actually a handy person to have around when you're dealing with someone like Agnes, who never runs out of crazy, seemingly impossible ideas, which often have you needing those odd bits of paraphernalia, like duct tape, or yarn, which is what we used to sew our coverings together.

Our coverings didn't impress Doug much either. Not really because we took the leaves off the trees in the front yard of Cherry Tree, but more because we wore the coverings to Walmart.

Considering that Agnes, Harriet, and Gertrude are adults in their seventies and eighties and are no strangers to burning their undergarments, they had a small bonfire in the front yard of the assisted living center, which my mom was called to put out.

If you've read my sisters' books, you know that my mom is the fire chief in Good Grief.

Of course, my mom being who she is, she didn't put the fire out but joined in the party, tossing her own undergarments on the blaze.

Since the fire company is all volunteer, she couldn't be fired.

Actually, it gave the town something to talk about for a good long while. Winter in Idaho can be long and hard, and people love having us give them something to talk about.

Everyone in town except for Doug.

But even he knows that we need to do something in order to attract new residents to Cherry Tree, or the place is going to close.

Agnes has the idea, and I have to agree, that if we're known as the hippest living center in the Northwest, people will want to retire here in droves.

I mean, come on, what does Florida weather have on a place where people make coverings, burn their undergarments, and go on whitewater rafting trips?

Okay, so we haven't actually gone on a whitewater rafting trip, but that's the plan.

Once I sweet-talk Doug into it.

That is Gertrude's idea. She feels like I need to put more honey in my interactions with Doug.

She always says, "You can catch more flies with honey than vinegar."

I, personally, don't have any idea why anyone would want to catch flies.

But Gertrude just smiles at me like she knows something I don't and suggests that I be nicer.

Then, of course, Agnes comes up with a crazy idea like this that I know is going to cost me my job and is certainly not going to get me any brownie points with Doug.

I think the only reason I haven't been fired already is because he hasn't been able to find anyone to take my place.

Good Grief isn't that big.

While the ladies are fun and I enjoy my job, they're known as somewhat of troublemakers around town.

We dump our bags of dirt on the pile, and Agnes straightens, a hand on her back.

I imitate her position and wonder how someone who's eighty can have so much energy.

"Hurt?" I ask her about her back, knowing that it must. Mine does.

"It does, but it's hurt for the last forty-five years, so this is nothing new."

Agnes looks young for eighty, but she still has those fine wrinkles around her eyes, and her face wreathes in a smile. The smile wrinkles are deep and pronounced because Agnes spends the majority of every day with that look on her face.

I wish I were half as happy.

When a person is hanging around Agnes, it's kind of hard not to be happy.

"That's a beautiful sunrise," she says, looking off to the east where the orange glow is melting with pink and blue above the mountains.

"It is indeed."

I've had plenty of jobs over the years, so I'm not entirely worried about this one, but I do like to be responsible. "That light is going to make it more likely that Doug will see us if he happens to drive by. Which I think he does every Saturday just to check up on us."

Agnes nods, a little bit of a twinkle in her eye. "You're right. We need to work faster." She hunches down. "And walk lower. Come on. Our hole is almost big enough for one of us to fit into it. If we work hard, all four of us might be able to get into it by this evening."

"Hey. I don't have to be in it. This is for you ladies," I say, although there is a part of me that thinks it would be fun to hang out with the ladies in their cave.

I know. This is not the type of thing that ladies typically enjoy doing, especially senior ladies. But Agnes, Gertrude, and Harriet are not your typical ladies.

Agnes shoots me a look that says I'm crazy. But she answers me anyway. "We are most definitely making it a four-person cave, even if we don't make it to China. I think, if we can fit four people into it, I can cross the China tunnel off my bucket list. My bucket list is so long I'm not sure I'm ever going to get to the end of it. I'll have to make some alterations, I believe."

I've never actually seen her bucket list, but she's not kidding about it. She has a lot of things on it.

We hurry back, scrunched over, with me wondering how in the world this lady does it.

I guess she grew up in a generation that wasn't afraid to work, and she's done it all her life.

You'd think she'd be happy to retire and play bingo and knit.

You'd think wrong if you thought that. Not Agnes.

We pass Gertrude and Harriet, scrunched over and carrying their bags of dirt, and Agnes hisses in a whisper, "Get down further! If Mr. Ridley drives by, he's going to be able to see us now that it's light. If I'm going to cross this off my bucket list, we've got to hurry. And we can't let him see us."

Harriet smiles, although it's kind of lost in the glow of her hair, which is reflecting the sunrise and is rather blinding. At least I don't have to worry about losing her. Not that I would. Agnes would never allow anyone on her team to get lost.

I think that's how she sees us at Cherry Tree. We're people on her team, everyone helping to knock off the items on her bucket list.

"Wait until you see how much dirt we got," Gertrude says, slightly less hissy and not quite as hunched over as we are.

That might cause Agnes some consternation, but it will not cause her to love them any less.

Agnes is fiercely loyal, and she and Gertrude and Harriet have been friends all their lives.

I'm a recent addition to their circle, but they've embraced me wholeheartedly.

Probably because I don't shut down their crazy schemes the moment they come up with them.

Regardless, if we're going to get this done, Agnes is right. We need to work quickly, and we can't let Doug see us.

You can continue reading by getting *Me and the Helpful Hurricane* HERE[1].

---

1. https://www.amazon.com/gp/product/B08WHSL5BW

Made in the USA
Columbia, SC
21 February 2025

54103340R00102